# Work and Community in the West

*the text of this book is printed*
*on 100% recycled paper*

# Work and Community in the West

## Edited by EDWARD SHORTER

94-1262

**HARPER TORCHBOOKS** ⸮
Harper & Row, Publishers
New York Evanston San Francisco London

A hardcover edition of this book is published by Harper & Row, Publishers, Inc.

First HARPER TORCHBOOK edition published 1973

LIBRARY OF CONGRESS CATALOG CARD NUMBER: 73-9079

STANDARD BOOK NUMBER: 06-131789-6 (PAPERBACK)

STANDARD BOOK NUMBER: 06-136110-X (HARDCOVER)

# Contents

# Work and Community in the West

# 1

# THE HISTORY OF WORK
# IN THE WEST:
## An Overview

### Edward Shorter

There was, once upon a time, such a thing as traditional society. What we have now and have had for the last fifty years or so is clearly modern society. And the social history of the West may be written as the story of how one gave way to the other. Everything changed. All the threads in the fabric of popular life were unraveled and then rewoven together: how people lived in families, how they interacted with their neighbors in communities, how they thought of the politically powerful.

A major cluster of threads in this reweaving is represented by work—how men and women earned their livelihoods. This book will present accounts of several different stages in the great transformation of work. But I ask the reader to bear in mind from the very outset that the specific story of work will be unintelligible—or meaningless—if it is not told in relationship to these other skeins in the process of modernization. Of course, changes in the *technology* of work can be presented without reference to anything else: how manual machines gave way to self-correcting "feedback" devices, how simple units for organizing production, such as the artisan's workshop, gave way to complex bureaucratic organizations, such as the factory. But this straightforward narrative has been told many times before and is, moreover, a bit on the dull side.

What is compelling in the story of work is how changes in the technology and organization of production brought forth changes in the lives of the individual workers and in the structure of the communities in which they lived. This is the story I should like to elaborate a bit in this brief introduction. We shall take in turn each of the three principal stages in the evolution of production, observing for each the precise form of work organization and the accompanying pattern of community life. I am not saying that a certain technology of production, such as skilled handwork in the artisanal system, *causes* a certain form of community organization, such as the guild system, to arise. I shall merely argue that first in Europe, and later to some extent in North America, certain kinds of productive organization marched hand in hand with certain forms of social and political life.

Let us classify systems of work on a simple, clear criterion: the scope they permit to human creativity and to the need for participation. We are taking, of course, as given that all people need to experience some measure of personal autonomy and to find to some extent an outlet for the spontaneity and originality of spirit with which nature has endowed them. The degree to which these mental properties force themselves into the forefront of consciousness depends on the individuals involved and on the cultures in which they live. But these qualities are among the few constants in the record of Western culture. And together they add up to the need for creative participation in whatever one happens to be doing. Because it happens in the West that people have spent, until recently, most of their waking hours at work, we may classify systems of work on how well they accommodate these human needs.

Now the story of changes in work in the West is the story of how one kind of system, based upon the creativity and autonomy of the individual producer, gave way to another kind

of system, based upon the subdivision of labor, the standardization of the finished product, and the turning of the worker
himself into a machine. Or, at least until recently, that was
thought to be the end of the tale. But within the last thirty years
some new developments in the history of work have started to
unfold, and so perhaps the provisional ending of the story will
be a happy one.

In the history of work, three distinct phases may be noted:

1. Artisanal work. The artisan is responsible for the production of a piece of merchandise from the beginning of the work
process to the end. He obtains the raw materials, designs the
product, and performs all the stages of production (or at least
all those requiring skill and judgment). Such a person must, it
goes without saying, understand the logic of the manufacture,
that is, the principles by which the raw materials take form in
consumer goods, the logic of advance from one phase of production to the next. Such a person will enjoy considerable latitude
for innovation and creativity, even though, unlike an artist, he
is working to the close specifications of a client. And such a
person will control the rhythms of his own work, the organization of his place of employ, the uses of his time. Thus several
different characteristics, centering on comprehension, participation, and control, combine to give this system of work its
uniqueness.

2. Industrial work. In the factory, the assembly-line worker
repeats a single task over and over again. He is told precisely
what to do, and is remunerated on the basis of his success in
conforming to those explicit directives. The industrialist's need
for efficient work dictates that the tasks be subdivided; modern
industry's need for interchangeable parts demands that the
work be standardized; and the assembly line's logic of unbroken
production requires that the worker sacrifice all control over
the rhythms of his own labor. Thus the factory system differs
from the artisanal system in that the worker loses his former
multivalent competency, his ability to do a number of different

tasks in the production of an object; he loses, of course, the opportunity to participate in what he's doing, to modify his product on the basis of some internal dialogue with himself; and he sacrifices control over the work situation, for what would happen to the profitability of a factory in which the workers were permitted to run about as they pleased, to take coffee breaks at will, or to decide at the spur of the moment that they didn't want to fashion pickup trucks at all but baby carriages instead?

(A small *caveat lector* at this point: The majority of jobs in modern industry are not, in fact, on assembly lines; nor, for that matter, are most jobs on the belt even in the archetypal automobile industry. But the assembly line represents a marvelous metaphor for repetitive, meaningless, alienating work, which is precisely what so many modern industrial jobs are. Even though most factory workers may not actually stand at the belt, their tasks are organized on principles of which the assembly line is merely the ultimate logical extension.)

3. Technological work. In very modern factories and bureaucracies, work is organized rather differently than in the dark satanic mill. Automation has created jobs calling for multicompetent employees, demanding of them a fundamental understanding of the factory's overall operation and of their particular role within it and permitting them a large measure of independence. This system of work has certain similarities with the old artisanal system, for it requires people who are highly trained and gives them great latitude in what they do, the difference being that their training is not acquired within the context of a professional organization, such as a guild, but rather off the job in technical schools and universities or, more commonly, on the job itself. Nor do "science-sector" workers possess the same realm of professional creativity that the old artisanal workers had, for the end products of the high technology plant must still be standardized. Technological work has some obvious traits in common with its predecessor, industrial work, too.

In both systems the worker finds himself within enormous bureaucracies, a small cog in a gigantic machine; in both systems as well, mechanization places the worker at several removes from direct engagement with the raw materials, at each remove reducing his ability to form the end product. But in contrast to the industrial worker, the employee of the science sector is likely to *try* for some measure of job control, molding in some way the forces that affect his destiny. Thus the high technology system of work represents a throwback to the artisanal system, yet with important modifications.

So these are three ways of organizing production, interesting in themselves yet absolutely intriguing to the student of history for the kinds of social organization that went with them. In the following pages we shall dwell heavily upon the world of values and social patterns which happened to exist alongside these technical systems of work. "Happened to exist" is too weak, of course, for the *kind* of work done affected without question the mentalities and social lives of the workers. Yet many other forces, independent of the system of work, came to bear as well upon these people. If we are to understand the guild, there are numerous aspects of the nature of early modern European society we must take up that have nothing to do with artisanal labor. If we are to understand the modern family or the modern city, we must discuss diffuse elements of contemporary life unrelated to assembly-line production. Technological determinism is as graceless as any other deterministic explanation, and the purpose of this introduction is to show that work mattered a little, but it was not the prime mover of modernization.

Finally, by way of preface, let us take a moment to clarify terms. "Traditional" society represents a well-defined period in Europe's social evolution, not just everything that came before the automobile. Exact dates vary, of course, from country to country, depending on when modernization began. But as a rule of thumb, "traditional" in England means the sixteenth to the early eighteenth century, in France from the sixteenth to the mid-nineteenth century, and in Germany from the six-teenth to the late nineteenth. In North America "traditional" society has never existed: Modern society sprang full-blown from the heads of the pioneers. The uniformity of the sixteenth-century "beginning" of the traditional period is partly an artifact of our ignorance of medieval social organization, partly a consequence of the Reformation itself. A number of scholars have argued brilliantly that after the sixteenth century we are, in terms of popular culture and values, playing in a new ball-game. But it is a game one is loath to call "modern" (even though convention calls for the French to do so), and to differentiate, therefore, this epoch of small-town solidarity from what came before and after, many North American scholars customarily employ the term "traditional." "Modern" means simply the years in which the great onrush of individualism began, in which the small community vanished.

## Artisanal Work

At once the two realms of our analysis—technical systems of work and forms of community organization—converge inseparably, for in traditional Europe artisanal work meant the guild system. No artisans existed without guilds, and no guilds without artisans, save for exotic exceptions. Called variously *corporations ouvrières, Innungen,* or "gilds," these organizations were responsible for the manufacture of most consumer goods between sometime in the High Middle Ages and the year 1800; the dates suggest the diffuseness of the guilds' beginnings and the abruptness of their demise.

Guilds existed for three ends: (1) to ensure high standards of competency and workmanship by regulating training, (2) to ensure a decent livelihood for their members by regulating the number of producers and the volume of goods they were permitted to turn out, (3) to represent their members in the marketplace of local political power by securing representation on the town council. To achieve this threefold task most guilds were outfitted with an array of public police powers. A man who wanted to make and sell shoes, to take a commonplace example, had to become a member of the shoemakers' guild, if he wanted to work in a town where such a guild was present. (Guilds for most consumer goods were to be found in most towns, less frequently in the countryside.) If the guildsmen did not want a competitor around, they could deny him membership and then drive him out of town, either through their own enforcement committee or through writ of the town council. Further, the guild could regulate the behavior of its own members, fining those whose work was substandard or, more frequently, those who took on too many journeymen, sold readymade goods in storefront shops, or otherwise threatened to impinge on the markets of their fellow guildsmen. Finally, the guild had a powerful say in municipal politics, for the town council might consist almost exclusively of craftsmen, entitled as such to seats. Or even if the guildsmen had no *de jure* representation in the local townhall, in practice the elders of the town would be largely artisans. The guild, it is clear, was much more than an institution for producing consumer goods through quaint hand methods.

A person who wanted to become an independent craftsman, which is to say, a guildsman, had to start young. When he had reached the age of fourteen or so, his relatives would pay a small fee to a master craftsman for taking the lad on. For the next three years the boy would live in the master's house, in theory learning by doing and watching done, in practice sweeping up the cutting room and carrying messages down to the "good old boys" in the local tavern. At age seventeen the apprentice would become a journeyman, leaving his initial master and going to another town or series of towns, to work in the employ of other masters. The guilds recognized within themselves a self-destructive tendency towards provincialism and technological stagnation, so they insisted that journeymen travel about, seeing how leather hides or ivory combs were produced in places far from their home towns. Upon returning, these journeymen would supposedly infuse new skills and energy into the moribund old hierarchy. The guilds also saw in journeymen a useful way of getting labor at less than market rates, for they insisted that every applicant spend some time in dependency, helping the master craftsman as a virtually full-fledged artisan while unable to strike out on his own. Finally, so the theory went, the barrel-maker journeyman would complete his own "masterpiece"; a local committee of senior barrel-makers would pass judgment on it, and if the piece were of acceptable quality, the young man would be admitted to the ranks of independent guildsmen, able to set up his own shop, to accept orders, to participate in local affairs, to get married (in some places the mastership was prerequisite for wedlock), and in turn to instruct other apprentices and journeymen in the craft of barrel making.

Consider the world of work of the guildsman. In an era of the most primitive mechanization, the only motive force was provided by his own body, the only machinery his own hands and a few simple tools which permitted him to manipulate directly the raw materials. He purchased his own supplies—leather, yarn, charring wood, or whatever. Aided customarily by no more than a single journeyman, he worked directly for his clients, transforming in a series of steps the raw material into finished goods: lumber into wagons, woolen cloth into Sunday suits, bars of wrought iron into door hinges and locks.

The rhythms of work were abrupt indeed. How misleading is the history primer's standard announcement that in times past "fourteen-hour days were not uncommon." Between the time the senior journeyman crossed the shop threshold in the morning and departed in the evening (often as not to ascend to his sleeping quarters in the garret of the master's house), fourteen hours might well elapse. But physical work, socializing, and play were so blended together within this time span that images of shoulders pressed continually to the wheel would be most inaccurate. Craftsmen worked slowly for one thing, unable to see any particular haste in any particular job. They worked intermittently for another, constantly changing tasks, stopping work, wheeling and dealing with the flow of people through the shop from outside. Finally, the work week was continually interrupted by religious holidays or punctuated by such craft traditions as "Blue Monday," on which journeymen didn't show up because either they were too hung over from Sunday or they wished to continue carousing. Precisely the point about sociability in the craft system is that work and leisure intermingled inextricably, so that the awareness of being part of a larger social community permeated the work place, and the awareness of belonging to an occupational community dominated social relations off the job.

Most of the old guildsmen would probably have agreed that several qualities of mind marked the good worker.

—Joy in the creativity of work. By this I mean something more than "pride in one's work." We may assume a flat feeling of disappointment in work poorly done to be another of those historic constants in Western society. What was limited to the guild system, however, was artistic embellishment as an expression of the joy of work itself. We are addressing a range of artisanal creativity which stretches from the scrollwork that wheelwrights would carve into finished wagons, through the decorative inlays that furniture makers would implace in table tops and bureaus, to the elaborate designs that master masons would mortar into the façades of buildings. Keep in mind that all these forms of creativity were severely defined by tradition, limiting the latitudes within which such individual expressiveness could move. The entire modern vocabulary of expressive behavior is risky in approaching these traditional people, for the entire social order and culture of which they were a part was based upon the *suppression* of spontaneity and individuality. Yet in the world of work, even in the small craft shops of remote provincial burgs, these qualities found an application.

—Doing work for its own sake, rather than as a means to some ulterior end. We are faced with two separate questions here: Why did people in fact work such long hours, and why did they think they worked so long? The economic compulsion to long working days is evident. In an era of low productivity, people had to spend an inordinate amount of time at work simply to earn a living. It takes only short bursts of employment in our high productivity economy to purchase a subsistence minimum. But in the Old Regime the same minimum could be acquired only through great investments of labor. So if work dominated the cultural world of traditional society, it was partly by necessity, for the economy could not sustain itself unless all hands were active for long, long hours.

Yet paradoxically the traditional worker justified his enterprise to himself in terms more moral and religious than economic. If asked, "Why do you work?" the craftsman would respond, "Because that's man's burden," or "Because God wills it." The modern worker, faced with the same question, would respond in a highly instrumental way: "To put a roof over my head," or "To live the good life." So an explanation of the centrality of work in the Old Regime must be nuanced, taking into consideration both what the external world made people do and what their own beliefs and mentalities persuaded them to do.

Traditional craftsmen were persuaded that work was good not necessarily because of the rewards it brought, but because the act of work itself permitted them to fulfill the principal social role the surrounding community had assigned to them: adhering to the dictates of tradition and custom. They worked as craftsmen because their fathers and grandfathers had been craftsmen. If a man became a cabinetmaker, it was because he came from a line of cabinetmakers, because everybody he knew expected him to follow that line, and because he would be able to find contentment in his small community only by doing what the rest of the community expected of him. This is what is meant by knowing one's place. The cabinetmaker spent his life turning out furniture in order to answer the question "Who am I?" not "Why do I work?" So in the bad old days doing work for its own sake was not a means of embarking on a voyage of self-exploration, as such phrases tend to suggest for modern people, but rather of mooring oneself to a fixed way of life.

—The sacrifice of individual advantage to community welfare. In the twentieth century we have enormous difficulty evoking this third quality of mind. Whereas we can, without too much trouble, imagine work which brings us into spontaneous creative contact with our raw materials and which we like so much that we do it for its own sake, regardless of the rewards, we find in the matter of individualism that we have the skins of leopards rather than of lizards. We simply cannot re-create for ourselves the moral universe of a society in which people believed implicitly that the success of the community came before the advantage of the individuals within it.

We are speaking of two kinds of communities, the narrow one of occupation itself (the guild) and the larger municipality in which the guild was situated. The guild craftsman saw himself as responsible to both varieties. He internalized the principle that he must not endanger the livelihood of his fellows in the pursuit of his own livelihood. If he were to employ more than the standard number of journeymen, say two, he would be able to undercut the prices of the other guild members through various economies of scale, and occupy an unfair share of the local market. If he were to experiment with ready-made wares, stockpiled in retail shops selling directly to the public, he would similarly reduce the total volume of business available to others. If he were to acquire the new machinery for, let us say, weaving which increasingly began its diffusion in the eighteenth century, he would again deny his colleagues business. What would become of these men and their families?

So the guildsman voluntarily refrained from taking on extra

2.5°° above
p.8

journeymen; he fulminated against the pack peddlers who ever more brought consumer goods from other regions into his local market; and he ignored technological innovations. The guild's police powers kept in line deviants whose sense of self overcame their obligations to the community. And it was only in the nineteenth century as the guild system lay dying, slain by the ax of the central state, that individual craftsmen in large numbers began that fundamental reorientation from community to competition with their colleagues.

Similarly, the guild craftsman was enmeshed in a set of ties to a larger residential community more resilient than his own self-interest. He had a powerful sense of place, so that the response, "I am a citizen of Memmingen," would vie strongly with the response, "I am a master tanner." Migration away in search of better-paying work or the pleasures of the big city was unthinkable for this stratum of population, in contrast to the lower classes who moved all over traditional Europe. And as long as poverty was seen in the master craftsman's moral universe as a curse of God rather than as a failure of character, he was willing to back—however grudgingly—municipal levies for the indigent or to give to the Church. Concern for the town's reputation rather than the spirit of Christian charity doubtless motivated this variety of sacrifice. But then, membership in the citizenry of the town was prominent in the self-identity of these men. We should not therefore be surprised to see them acting in favor of the collectivity; they were, in the last analysis, acting in support of themselves.

What I have written about the moral universe and mechanics of the guild system is as much a statement of what its members wanted to think of themselves as a description of the reality of their lives. Actual practice often departed from the ideal type I have sketched. It is especially important that we keep track of the people who didn't fit into the guild system, and of those who were victimized by it, in order to understand the nature of work in traditional Europe.

Many men and women suffered from the breakdown of the guild system's own rules. One time-honored rule, for example, said that every qualified apprentice who entered at the bottom had a mastership waiting at the top. Already before the eighteenth century this rule had started to collapse in larger cities, but the general population growth of the eighteenth century put it in question everywhere. The number of bodies clamoring for jobs in the guild system was simply growing more rapidly than the ability of the economy to create extra posts. Thus many men found themselves in the status of journeymen for life, all chance of becoming masters barred. The guilds claimed that even the existing masters had trouble making ends meet, to say nothing of creating new ones.

Another time-honored rule said that guildsmen would not impinge on one another's territory or impair one another's independence. But after the middle of the eighteenth century, changing technology began to shift the conditions of supply, and new consumer tastes, along with increasingly complex markets, began to alter the demand side of guild economics. In furniture making and the garment industry, for example, mass markets with modish tastes worked against the little craftsman, who had not the wit to stay abreast of new fashions nor the capital to handle large orders. Only a few ambitious artisans were able to borrow money for modern machinery, to learn to deal with wholesalers, and to mass-produce cheap, attractive wares for fickle consumers. These men then proceeded to employ their less fortunate former colleagues. Where formerly in many industries had been a band of brothers now existed two distinct social classes, the *gens de bien* and the *gens de rien*.

A final derogation from the standards of the past was the deterioration of artisanal competency, especially among rural craftsmen. In the golden age of the guild system many workers may in fact have possessed the dynamic creativity and will to excellence described above, but by the eighteenth century both customers and government officials were complaining loudly about wares that were substandard, shoddy, dirty, and indifferently produced. The guild system in theory had nothing against the improvement of the art, as long as it progressed evenly across the board. But in reality any innovation upon age-old practices came to be regarded suspiciously by these anxious provincials.

We must also remember that some important sectors of the traditional economy were not organized by the guilds. Some of those sectors were characterized by artisanal mentalities; some were not.

There were no guilds for farmers, of course, for most of them were peasants. But the communitarian nature of agriculture in many parts of Europe evoked some of the conditions of work and frames of mind common to artisans. Agriculture involves, for example, the same dynamic interaction with the soil that the craftsman experiences with his raw materials. The peasant must similarly have some notion of the logic of the work process. The same challenging variety of tasks is present, the same need to adjust to changing conditions. Only in agriculture it is nature and not the customer that changes the conditions. In those areas of Europe—principally the northwest—where peasant dwellings were grouped into nuclear settlements rather than dispersed in hamlets, a communitarian sentiment comparable to the corporate spirit of the guildsmen seems to have held neighbors together. In the winter a number of families would gather in someone's cowbarn, profiting from the warmth of the livestock, to spin or knit and to tell tales—an institution referred to as the *veillée* in France, the *Spinnstube* in Central Europe. And although land was owned individually, the fields in which these little strips were located were often subject to communal control so that collective decisions were made over land use and the cycle of cropping. Such communitarian agricultural arrangements are far closer to the artisanal guild in spirit than to the individualistic capitalism of twentieth-century farming.

There were two principal areas where the creative involvement and the occupational polyvalence of artisanal work were

*not* the rule. First, there was the agricultural laborer, whom
Edwin Markham captured in the famous lines, "Bowed by the
weight of centuries he leans upon his hoe. . . ." The particular
hand that snuffed out the light within that brain was deadening,
grinding field labor, done at the behest of the farmer. Many
people were employed in such jobs, wherever in Europe large-
scale agriculture, needing a casual work force, was to be found.
There was no "dynamic participation in the work process" for
these people, and the almost complete absence of field-laborer
revolts in European history testifies to a lacking corporate consciousness.

Second, artisanal work and the guild spirit were absent where
modern industry had begun to take hold in the countryside. It
is not commonly recognized that the first great leap forward in
Europe's industrial growth came not in urban factories but in
rural cottages, in the form of the "putting out system," the
"domestic system," or quite simply "cottage industry." Urban
entrepreneurs would dispatch raw materials to peasant homes
in the nearby hinterland, sending, for example, raw cotton out
to be spun into yarn, then giving the yarn to another group of
outworkers to be woven into cloth, then finally having the
finishing done in the city and expediting the yard goods to
distant markets. The peasants had spinning wheels and looms
right in their cottages. They worked at piece rates. Nail making,
glove sewing, cutlery manufacture, and basket weaving were
among the many facets of the vast tableau of rural industry
which had arisen by 1800. In every part of Europe a proletariat
of cottagers had been set to the work of modern industry. At its
apogee the system came to involve an enormous number of
people, perhaps as many as one in every three rural dwellers.

Interesting for our purposes is the nature of the work. Cottage industry marks the initial eruption of modern work techniques, for it involved a high degree of specialization of labor
along with rational procedures for marketing and accounting.
This was the spirit of capitalism, with which for the first time

large numbers of common people came into contact. In their daily lives it meant the needless repetition of a few standardized tasks, the pounding out of nailheads, the continuous twisting of the roving in spinning, the benumbing needlework of lace making. There was no variety, no creative participation. This was industrial work.

## Industrial Work

We must not be too quick to speak of "the factory," for the historic turning point between artisanal and industrial systems came not with the physical lodgment of production in factory buildings, but with the subdivision of labor. It was first in rural cottage industry that parceled work commenced. Only much later on the threshold of the twentieth century was the assembly line to import this principle of subdivided production into the factory. In early factories for printing presses or pumping machinery, for example, most of the workers were highly skilled artisans, handling multiple tasks, engaging creatively with new problems of production which surfaced almost daily. From the viewpoint of technical labor, therefore, the factory itself is not a significant landmark.

Before we see exactly what difference the factory *did* make, however, we must deal with one massive exception to the rule of skilled workers in early industrialization—the textile industry. Textile mills employed from the very beginning an unskilled work force. Mechanization in spinning and weaving had been introduced precisely to make skilled labor unnecessary. It is true that textile mills employed a significant proportion of the labor force, but not one of sufficient importance to warrant the attention this industry has received in standard accounts. Historians have been transfixed by the Sadler Report in England or by Louis-René Villermé's account of conditions in the French textile industry. The case of textiles has literally blotted out our view of other industrial sectors, and because its work system was virtually unique among factories of the time, our general image of early industrial technology has been severely dis torted. This distortion is partly Marx's fault, for he fixed upon the English cotton industry as the prototype of capitalist indus- trial growth. The reality turned out to be considerably more complex.

The steam engine reduced somewhat the artisanal compo- nent of factory work, yet did not extinguish it. Tools run by machine were, after all, more powerful but not fundamentally different in nature from hand tools. Human skill and judgment would continue to breathe life into factory machinery until the development of "feedback" servomechanisms which adjusted themselves automatically.

It was the assembly line that represented the great divide between artisanal and industrial systems of work. The purpose of the line was to permit each worker to accomplish just one task, thereby accelerating production and downgrading skill levels (and homogenizing pay differentials). As the economics of production were to have it, belt-line workers turned out to make higher wages than most other kinds of factory workers, but consider what they lost:

1. They sacrificed control over the rhythms of the work pro- cess, for the pace of the line determined the pace of the job. And liberation from the line for a toilet break or a stroll would come only with the utility man's arrival or the halting of the line itself.

2. They sacrificed an overview of the work process. The wheelnut screwers-on in an automobile plant need understand nothing of the process of manufacturing automobiles nor of their own role in it. They did simply as they were told, unaware of what had gone before their post, what came after, or why. Their work ceased to be meaningful, in the literal sense of the term.

3. They sacrificed participation in the work process, for the

realm of choices over which they could autonomously decide shrank virtually to zero. There were no problems on the line, no decisions to be taken. Their value to the company, indeed, would be measured in the extent to which they succeeded in putting to sleep that part of the brain that craves involvement and control.

So the assembly line was the kiss of death for the artisanal spirit. Yet even before its advent, even before the Taylors and the Gilbreths of "scientific management" had begun their human engineering, other aspects of factory work had written "finis" to the guild mentality.

At this point we pass from technical systems of work to the realm of social organization itself. If the assembly line meant the transition from artisanal to industrial work modes, other dimensions of factory life ended that whole constellation of community organization resting upon the guild. The basis of worker sociability shifted in the factory from the guild to the labor union or entirely away from the plant itself to large territorial units.

Even in early factories, with all their polyvalent work routines, guild organization would have been impossible. Three elements of the work situation essential to guild solidarity had been lost in the dark, satanic mill: worker independence, small industrial scale, and labor force stability. The secret of the guild's endurance through the ages had been stability and intimacy: a small band of fellows who had known each other all their lives and whose sons would in the same way be comrades. A larger group of associates would inevitably have taken on a paler complexion; a less stable band of buddies would have interacted differently. The factory was both large and unstable. A metalsmith at Le Creusot (heart of the Schneider weapons empire in France) would be thrown together with many other metalsmiths, far more than he would have encountered in the little metalsmith's guild of nearby Autun, say, in the Old Regime. And these men would come and go, here one day, gone the next, depending on their personal whimsy and on the arbitrary will of the employer—both factors which were vastly reduced in the "good old days" when there were no employers and the ties of community reached out to minimize the role of individual arbitrariness. So in the big factory the very givens of social contact among the work force would differ from the scattering of small craft shops of the Old Regime: you saw less of your fellows, and you had less of a stake in dealing with them, because who knew if they'd be around tomorrow.

The third difference between factory and craft shop social organization—worker independence—is slightly more complex. As we have seen, guildsmen were of considerable political importance in their local communities under the Old Regime. They acquired this stature by virtue of membership in the town's *Bürgertum*, that stratum of property-holding independent citizens for whom no man was master. Factory workers, however well paid, had sacrificed the essential criterion—independence—for local participation in small polities. They were beholden to an industrialist, a man who at any minute for reasons known only to himself, or indeed "just for no reason at all," might let them go. In nineteenth-century Europe, economic independence continued to be so highly prized that those who had lost it fell from the municipal political class. Now, as we have seen, one of the guild's principal reasons for being was to organize the political and cultural life of the small town. But once former guildsmen (or their children) gave up this criterion for political participation, the organizations which formerly had represented them so ably in the town council now lost stature in the eyes of the other citizens. Nineteenth-century urban politics took on new organizational foundations and devolved upon a new political class. The guilds had been expelled from the polity.

Thus the factory assaulted the artisan's world from at least two quarters. The first attack came across the lines of technical systems of work: the scope of participation and autonomy the job itself offers. The factory chiseled away at these qualities in various measures until the 1890s, when the widespread adoption of parceled production caved in the remainder of artisanal work modes. The second attack was launched across the sector of social organization, for the factory annihilated the artisans' rationale for solidary collective life and for political influence. When the smoke had finally cleared and the full dimensions of the "social question" been realized, it became evident that a former class of essentially bourgeois producers had been ground down to the status of proletarians, alienated and disinherited.

What new forms of associational life did these proletarians forge for themselves? Reflect for a moment on the kinds of organization they did *not* need. Unlike the guildsmen, these industrial workers did not require organizations for occupational training and professional perfection. The proletarians had no special skills, no trade secrets, no arts that one could acquire only intuitively through long and intimate association with masters of the trade. They themselves were without skills, save those learned on the job or in brief training courses in technical schools. So their organizations would lack all the sentimental and institutional apparatus that goes with transmitting knowledge from generation to generation.

Unlike the guildsmen, these industrial workers did not require organizations stressing sociability and professional consciousness. So many ties bound together the old artisans: the common bonds of doing exactly the same métier, a sense of defending collective interests, the friendship ties that close contact across the years and generations nurture. No wonder that the professional "corporation" constituted the emotional center of the artisan's world, around which everything else rotated. Very little needed rotate about the proletarian's organization, for he had little in common with his fellows. He had in all likelihood not known them for long. Even though he probably did the same thing as countless other wheelnut screwers-on, he felt little emotional solidarity with them. Screwing on wheel-nuts was, after all, not such a big thing, a job learned in five minutes and forgotten as soon as the worker walked through the factory gates; there were certainly no professional interests involved in screwing on wheelnuts, for the job couldn't get any worse, any more brainless and boring than it already was, and so no occupational privileges existed to be defended.

The only thing the proletarian had in common with his fellows was a consciousness of class, an awareness of being exploited, of being at the bottom of a system of economic organization that rewarded him and his mates in shockingly unjust disproportion to their contribution. But this variety of class consciousness is, after all, a rather intellectual kind of process. The proletarian must think through a series of simple equations in order to conclude that he is receiving less than his fair share and that equity will come only through a fundamental judicial modification of his relationship to the means of production. Awareness of membership in an industrial proletariat, as an abstract *prise de conscience,* bears little in common with the visceral ties of affect holding together guildsmen.

The organizations of the new industrial proletariat had, therefore, certain singular features:

—Their programs were all instrumental, designed to obtain some objective for their members in the exterior world rather than to facilitate association for expressive, affective purposes. Like industrial work, industrial unionism was a means to an ulterior end, not an end in itself. The labor unions, occupational self-help societies, cooperative associations of industrial workers became transfixed, to be exact, by the end of obtaining political power at the center of the nation-state.

—Their structure was highly bureaucratized and centralized, tending to unify local organizations in pyramids with very pointed tops. Unions quickly developed national and international hierarchies, and local autonomy was much less important than central control. The guilds, it goes without saying, had been the embodiment of localism. Although they sometimes possessed national organizations, where the political authorities would permit them, the center of the guildsman's universe was very much his own community.

—Although cast into bureaucratic steel at the top, modern unions were highly unstable at the bottom, the direct opposite of the guild pattern. Workers drifted in and out; attendance at meetings was poor. Membership indifference to local organizations soon became notorious, the despair of organizers on both sides of the Atlantic. The French unions, for example, had to struggle heroically to get even a small percentage of the workers in a given plant to pay dues. The only issues that seemed to arouse passion, or which at least permitted the simultaneous mobilization of large numbers of workers, were national political questions.

The contrast could not be drawn more sharply. The old professional corporations were tenaciously localistic, commanded firm allegiance from their members, and served to transmit an entire way of life and an established political position across the gulch of time. Industrial worker organizations, of which labor unions overshadowed all rivals, soared toward a central apex in great bureaucratic arcs, had little place in the emotional commitments of their members, and were much more concerned with the acquisition of national political power than with the transmission across time of any particular set of skills and traditions.

This characterization fits industrial unionism better than craft, but in the West craft unions have drifted steadily toward the model of industrial unionism, away from their historic guild inheritances. Marx's contempt for "worker elites" was to prophesy the future.

Now, of course, there are other answers to the question of why by the year 1947 every nation-state in the West had a centralized, stratified, coordinated worker movement. Changes in the nature of work itself are by no means the sole explanation of this phenomenon. One must point to the growth of very big cities, the centralization of political power through the nation-state, the advent of continentwide communications media, and other factors as well. I am saying merely that the transformation of the technical system of work through mechanization, professional dequalification, increases in industrial scale, and a Taylorist emphasis upon shop-floor discipline and efficiency played an important role.

But all members of the modern labor force are not in factories. One of the hallmarks of economic growth since the turn of the twentieth century has been a relative shift away from the manufacturing sector toward the services sector. Do these arguments about the causes and consequences of change in work apply to this burgeoning group of service workers, clerks, delivery men and elevator operators? In a word, yes.

Many writers have noted the same subdivision of tasks, the same loss of professional autonomy among the white-collar and service workers that went on among the factory proletariat. Indeed, we would not stretch things to speak in the first half of the twentieth century of a white-collar proletariat. Once upon a time most white-collar jobs represented an extension of managerial authority and thus involved exercising control, being autonomous, and so forth. The job of the nineteenth-century clerk, for example, was multifaceted, responsibile, and avidly desired. Such early white-collar workers were close to being intellectuals ("clerc" in French, used to mean intellectual among other things) and, therefore, close to artisanal work systems. The explosion of white-collar employment in the government services, banking, insurance, and the great corporations brought workers whose jobs were an extension of the manual laborer's position rather than of the employer's. The telephone operator, the insurance clerk, the level-crossing attendant all performed repetitive tasks without participation or the chance of creativity. Their jobs were thoroughly mechanical. As soon as technology lurched another step or two forward after the

Second World War, these people started to be replaced, in fact, by machines.

What kinds of organizations did these proletarians in white collars fashion for themselves? They stayed largely away from professional associations. Or if they did establish their newsletters and burial funds from time to time, they certainly shunned militant collective action. The white-collar proletariat failed for a long time to awaken to its actual status, refusing to believe that it was a new working class rather than a new managerial class. In the world view of white-collar workers during perhaps the years 1850–1950, the occupations of clerk or salesman were "respectable," which means on the side of the politically powerful rather than on that of the powerless. And "respectable" people don't strike or riot or combine against their employers. They shouldn't have to if they're already close to the seat of national political power.

One of the longest double takes in history was to come in the industrial West in the 1950s and 1960s as this white-collar proletariat realized that it wasn't on the side of the influential at all and that there was nothing inherently undignified about collective action. One has to look out for oneself after all. At this writing the efforts of white-collar workers to forge for themselves militant labor unions, exactly along the lines of industrial worker unions, is among the most fascinating developments in the study of work.

A final note on the organizational world of industrial work. I have perhaps left the impression, so common in modern sociological writing, that industrial workers are without close affective ties to other people or to collective activities, that they represent the disaffiliated, disorganized modern person, floating rootlessly through the chaos of modern society. That impression would be entirely inaccurate.

But before proceeding, the reader should be reminded that these matters are all highly speculative. And what is riskiest of all is not a reconstruction of the guild system and its members' beliefs but a portrait of the factory system. The history of the fabric of popular life in the nineteenth and early twentieth centuries is a great uncharted frontier of historical research. We have a sense of the artisan's world, and we certainly know from contemporary sociological surveys the worker's world of today. But what came in between is unknown country. Exactly what did happen to peasants and small-town artisans once they migrated to the big city or to the sprawling suburban metalworking plant? Who were their friends? What kinds of associations did they join? From whom did they take their cues for cultural and political beliefs? The lives of these industrial workers, so near to us in time, are far removed in understanding. The basic record has still not yet been pieced together.

Yet a few statements about industrial workers and their community life seem justifiable. I would argue that the family replaced the professional association as the principal institution binding the worker to the life of the larger community. The union, unlike the guild, became emotionally neutral for the industrial worker, an instrument for fattening his paycheck rather than for extending his personality. In his world the family acquired the strongest emotional charge.

The simultaneity in the transformation of work and of family life is not happenstance. Exactly at the time the *Stammtisch* (a nice German expression for the "good old boys' " corner at the local tavern) was disintegrating, the modern nuclear family was emerging. This is another story, the telling of which would spring the framework of this introduction. Suffice it to say that in traditional society the inward-looking, cloistered, nuclear family was incompatible with strong ties between individual and small town. Domesticity would have short-circuited the wiring of the little community, reducing the allegiance of individuals to the commonweal in the measure that it snuggled them closer to the bosom of family life.

In sixteenth- and seventeenth-century Europe the community had intervened at many points in family dynamics, meddling shamelessly in what was later to become an inviolable sphere of privacy. The small-town community was closely involved in child raising, via the custom of exchanging children as servants, via elaborate networks of godparentage, and via the little community's collective interest in socializing those who were to become its members in the ways of politeness, obedience, respect, and so forth. Examples of such customs as calling older women "aunt" come immediately to mind. The community intervened in family life with *charivaris, Haberfeldtreiben,* "rough music," or "chivarees," as was called in various languages and places the custom of noisily demonstrating before the home of someone who had violated community standards of comportment. In these ceremonies the villagers would subject to ridicule men who permitted themselves to be henpecked by their wives or older widows who were taking young men as husbands. These *charivaris* customarily entailed a whole assortment of costumes, rituals, and mock punishments (such as forcing the miscreant to ride backward on a donkey or to don a set of horns if he were being reproached as a cuckold) for offenses against the regular operation of the mating market and the prescribed norms of family life. Finally, the village community intervened in the organization of courtship; in some parts of Europe young men and women would get to know one another principally through festivals or knitting evenings supervised by the assembled villagers; in other places mating would be done within the context of formal organizations of young people. Such, at all events, was the interrelationship between family and community in traditional society.

The families of industrial workers appear to have differed significantly from these traditional families, which had been open at all sides to community interaction. Courtship was withdrawn from the purview of the community, becoming an intimate transaction conducted in privacy between two individuals. The *foyer,* or family hearth, became a private shrine to domesticity, in which Mama, Papa, and the two children gathered to celebrate tenderness and affection. Domestic quarrels were no longer mediated by anyone save, in desperate cases, the state. Thus the shutters were drawn, the outside world excluded from the newly privatized world of family life.

Although domesticity and privacy came to characterize many kinds of families in the nineteenth century, involved in various forms of livelihood, I believe there to have been a special relationship between industrial work and the sentimental family. Romantic love represents the emotional core of the modern nuclear family, and essential to this variety of sentiment is a powerful sense of one's own self-identity. Only people who are highly conscious of their own personal needs and desires, who have an explicit awareness of where *ego* stops and the outside community begins, are adapted for romantic love. The industrial system was calculated precisely to instill this sense of *amour-propre* among those caught up in it. Modern capitalism encouraged privatization partly through its organization of free markets on the principle of self-interest and the maximization of individual advantage, partly through fragmenting the work community and leaving the individual worker the sense that he was accomplishing productive tasks solely for the purpose of maintaining a roof over himself and his family.

Perhaps I am wrong about the sources of romantic love. But I believe that my characterization of the new nuclear family as a social unit held together by sentiment is perfectly just. Romantic love, rather than the parents of the bride and groom, came to call the changes in the mating dance. And young worker couples believed too, if only for a while, that the reason they were together was because they loved each other.

Thus a change in systems of work contributed to a change in community organization. The nuclear family interposed itself in the formerly direct relationship between individual and little community. Community institutions took on increasingly the aspect of what sociologists call "secondary associations"; the family became, increasingly, the sole "primary" association in the social order. With the professional corporation (the guild) no longer viable, the entire structure of sociability which had rested upon it became untenable. And in a brave new world of machines and efficiency experts, workers retreated to new little communities of three and four where they felt at home.

## The Science Sector

Marx would have been completely confounded by changes in the nature of work since the Second World War. Writing in the middle of the last century, he saw industrial skill levels dropping. At a time when mechanization meant machine tending, Marx thought the labor force would tend to become ever more homogeneous, more and more workers doing jobs increasingly brainless and simplified. For a long time he was right, as I have suggested in discussing factory industrial work. But events since approximately 1945 have gone in exactly the opposite direction.

The application of sophisticated theories of electronics and chemistry to industrial production seems to have initiated a new phase in the history of work. Across a wide front of manufacturing, and in the services sector too, jobs have become increasingly complicated, demanding substantial formal education and the exercise of a wide range of intellectual faculties. The technology which contemporary industry began to acquire in the 1950s and 1960s was in fact so complicated that the men and women who ran it had to become more like old-style artisans than proletarian machine-tenders. They had jobs requiring the exercise of initiative, a sense of responsibility, and occasionally creativity. The systems analyst, the laboratory technician, the refinery panel-monitor, the telephone line repairman: such jobs constituted admittedly, a minority of the total number of positions within the total labor force, but it was a growing minority, and the commonplace assembly-line and ditch-digger jobs were becoming fewer. In the United States warnings grew shriller against dropping out of high school before acquiring a marketable skill (or diploma); in Europe the revolution of the *cadres* and "Die Executiven" was celebrated.

Marx couldn't have foreseen the technological revolution within industry. In 1850 he had no way of realizing that in 1950 the practical application of theoretical scientific knowledge would *upgrade* levels of qualification within the work force, reversing the long deterioration of skill that had created the factory proletarians. But that is precisely what petro-this, aero-that, and cyber-the-other had accomplished. The wheelnut screwer-on in Detroit continued to dominate public thinking about manufacturing, but in fact such assembly-line workers were declining in proportion.

May we therefore speak of the new artisans, polyvalent skilled workers in white coats rather than leather aprons? Was the wheel of work rolling back to its starting point of talented, dedicated people, the center of whose world was a dynamic interaction with the materials of nature? Yes and no.

First, what the science-sector workers have in common with the old craftsmen.

—Science-sector employees participate actively in their work, as did the old guild artisans. Problems arise in the electricity transmission station; the employees have to diagnose the difficulty by reading the dials and then act to correct it. A simple problem, comparable perhaps to making shoes for a pair of especially large feet: in both cases there are general guidelines about sole stitching or circuit breaking, but in both cases the application of general knowledge to a specific set of facts demands mental agility and a sense of judgment, the preconditions of participation. For what the individual worker decides in each case will make a big difference in the product's outcome, whether the shoes pinch or the city goes black.

—Science-sector workers enjoy a substantial measure of

autonomy in two senses. They have control over their jobs so that no one lacking their special professional competence can intervene without their permission. And they have control over their work rhythms and patterns, deciding among themselves when they will do what. The workers at the generator station may well set collegially their own work routines and schedules, secure in responding to inquisitive supervisory personnel, "Look, who's doing this job, you or me?" This is, approximately, the way things were in Ye Olde Shoe Shoppe.

—Finally, science-sector workers resemble guildsmen in their high levels of professional solidarity. Shoptalk is not a sociable problem among proletarians; it is within science-sector gatherings. Missile engineers and desk-calculator repairmen tend to see one another much more frequently off the job than do refrigerator assemblers. There runs across the entire front of technological advance a spirit of professional community that has every counterpart in the "world we have lost," little in the dark, satanic mill.

But before we rush to embrace these technicians and professionals as the guildsmen of the twentieth century, let us consider as well some weighty differences.

—Science-sector workers have high levels of formal education, rather than an intuitive sense of craft absorbed through long years of practice. Or else they learn their jobs through formal company training programs. Neither form of initiation has the power to solder individuals in the matrix of association which the advancement from apprentice to journeyman to master gave the guilds.

—Job skills in the science sector are not transferable from one kind of plant to another, in contrast to the skills of, say, a carpenter or a metalsmith. The old craftsmen were supposed to be competent in a wide range of specific jobs (although later fragmentation of craft work among related guilds violated in practice this principle of multicompetency). The modern technician is bound to a specific product line or function, and dismissed oil refinery workers cannot easily switch over to rubber-processing plants. The universality of a craft skill gave its possessor an independence the modern technician simply does not have.

—Although opportunities for initiative and spontaneity characterize the science sector, there is in fact little scope for creative work. The end products must be standardized, the job specifications are closely written. The computer programmer does not leave his signature on a tabulation in the same manner that a brickmason left his on the façade of a building. The programmer's work is noticed by others only if it's erroneous. There's only one right answer at the insurance company but many lovely ways to frame a window in stone. Here the positive forces of job enlargement collide head-on with the exigencies of modern business. One may, as the Swedish have done, experiment with participation and worker control in giving small groups the responsibility of putting together cars; but the Volvos that emerge at the end all have to be the same.

—The sense of place in the social order is lacking. One reason why people found it so gratifying to be carpenters or saddlers was that everybody in the small town knew what their job was, and thought highly of them for following custom and tradition, as one was supposed to. Doing jobs that had a fixed place in the order of things gave their holders a fixed sense of place as well in this social hierarchy. There was no anxiety about social position, no anxious looking back and asking, "How am I doing, ma?" because these people received community recognition precisely for not changing, for doing things as they had always been done. People do not like movement and mobility and confusion in traditional society. This is why adherence to custom and avoidance of innovation weighed so heavily in the guild system. Because in their specific work roles the craftsmen discovered their places in a larger social order, a society which they and those about them considered changeless.

Such community reinforcement is missing from the work

satisfactions of the service sector. Neighbors and fellow citizens may know what someone does for a living, but that will be much less important to them than his other attributes, such as education, life style, income, and position of power within the social order. So all the gratifications that go with confidence in one's position are lost for the modern worker, *as far as his work is concerned*. Because nobody really cares what he does.

There are no sets of rules for social behavior that accompany modern jobs. Knowing what your neighbor does gives you, at most, a clue of what life style to expect from him, how many cars (in Europe whether a car at all), the completeness of the carpeting, the nature and frequency of drinks before dinner. Knowing what your neighbor does gives you little sense of whether the rules of the social game will be followed or even of what the specific rules are. What will the Imperial Oil technician next door do if his son gets your daughter pregnant? What will be his response toward his son, your daughter, and you? In the bad old days the answers to these questions would have been easily predictable within any given small town, although the specific answers might well have differed from one region to another.

A culture is a set of rules for social behavior and a mental table of the chances that a given signal concerning a given rule from one of the participants in the culture will produce an expected response among the other participants. In traditional Europe occupations were the principal means of keeping track of the signals. So a knowledge of what one's neighbor did for a living was fundamental. In the twentieth century we have, to no less an extent, reliable rules for cultural operations. But occupation is much less important as a means of keeping track of what particular set is in play and what the chances are of the rules being followed.

To sum up, the commonalities between science-sector workers and the old artisans may well produce similarities in behavior at work. If modern technicians and professionals truly turn

out to have the same sense of collective pride, the same need
for participation and autonomy in their work, that the old artisans had, some important changes in the design of jobs and
perhaps indeed in labor militancy may be in the offing. Because,
as we have seen, both groups feel strong emotional involvement
in their work and are prone to express sharp disapproval if their
expectations are not met. But modern technicians stand in a
fundamentally different relationship to community life than did         X
the old guildsmen. It was this intimate link between work and
community that gave the world we have lost its integrity. And
I think it unlikely that we shall see it again.

# 2

# HOMETOWNS AND GUILDS IN EARLY MODERN GERMANY

## Mack Walker

In conversation once, Walker seemed surprised that I thought his book so important. After all, he said, it's just an overview of German institutional history in a period forgotten by all but a handful of pedants. As a specialist, of course, he knew the times and people so well that he had long ceased to be amazed at their singularity within the long sweep of Western history. Looking in more from the outside, I was captivated by the community arrangements these hometowners had developed for doing social and economic business. But what intrigued me most was the success of the guilds in "smothering" conflict and in exacting the loyalty of their members. If by community we mean the readiness of individuals to subordinate the pursuit of private goals and gratifications to the maintenance of the commonweal, these German small towns in the years from around 1640 to 1820 were the real thing. It has become fashionable within sociology to debunk the old *Gemeinschaft-Gesellschaft* (community-society) distinction of Ferdinand Tönnies, but it is clear to me in reading Walker's book that the little towns of early modern Germany came as

SOURCE: Mack Walker, *German Home Towns: Community, State, and General Estate, 1648–1871* (Ithaca, N.Y.: Cornell University Press, 1971), pp. 73–86, 102–107. Reprinted by permission of Cornell University Press. Footnotes omitted.

close to being genuine "Gemeinschaften" as any secular structure is likely ever to have come. The discussion of the guilds which I have reprinted here shows how the economic institutions of the workaday world were embedded within this larger social order.

Walker currently teaches history at Cornell University. His first book was a study of German emigration overseas in the nineteenth century.

The tinsmith Flegel, citizen of Hildesheim, was in love, and he wished to marry. That he should marry was in itself seemly, for the proper pursuit of his trade required a solid domestic establishment supporting and surrounding the workshop: a wife to help out and meet customers, and to provide relatives; a decent home for apprentices and a gentling influence on journeymen; an assurance of Flegel's own diligence and reliability as a valuable member of the community. The trouble was that Flegel had set his heart, not wisely but too well, on the daughter of a fellow citizen named Helmsen; and when he went to register his intention to marry with the tinsmith's guild he was barred from doing so on grounds of indecency. The prospective bride's father—not she herself—had been born out of wedlock and then subsequently legitimized, whether by the belated marriage of his parents or by special government decree does not appear. At any rate Helmsen's legitimacy was recognized by the territorial law of the Bishopric of Hildesheim, in which the community was located, but that did not make him legitimate in the eyes of the Hildesheim guildsmen. Indeed the citizen status of the sometime bastard Helmsen suggests that outside influence had forced him on the community, ensuring the unending rancor of the real Hildesheimer. The guild constitution, to which Flegel had subscribed, provided that wife as well as master must show proof of four irreproachable grandparents; and inasmuch as a master's children were automatically eligible for guild acceptance and support, Flegel's determination to marry the Helmsen girl demanded of the tinsmiths that they sponsor the grandchildren of a bastard before the community.

Flegel had become engaged in 1742. Eleven years before, in 1731, an imperial edict had appeared which provided, among other things, that legitimacy established by "the authorities" should be recognized as valid by the guilds. Accordingly Flegel appealed to the Hildesheim Town Council against the guild decision, citing the imperial decree. But who were the authorities in Hildesheim? The important guilds of the town were directly and constitutionally involved in town government, ostensibly as representative of the citizenry: the *Ämter* of the butchers, the bakers, the shoemakers, the tanners, and the *Gilden* of the tailors, the smiths, the wool weavers, the retailers, and the furriers. Moreover the first four, the *Ämter*, had a special relation with the bishop which they used as leverage against the Council when they felt need of it. The Council therefore (it seems to have been an unusually flabby body to boot) turned the case over to its committee for artisans' affairs; and there nothing was decided. After a year, Flegel took the extraordinary step of marrying Fräulein Helmsen anyway, in a ceremony held somewhere outside Hildesheim. When the guildsmen heard of it they were enraged; never before, they said, had a Hildesheim master artisan thus defied his guild's jurisdiction in marital matters. For Flegel to get away with it would violate one of the most important sanctions the guild had for controlling the composition and the behavior of its membership. And it would make the Hildesheim tinsmiths look bad, and with them all the other Hildesheimer. The guild excluded Flegel from its meetings and functions, and it goes without saying that it imposed economic and social boycott against him, master tinsmith though he was.

For three years, Flegel appeared repeatedly before the Town Council asking that the imperial decree be enforced in his favor; repeatedly he was turned away. In 1745 he appealed to the episcopal govennment, declaring that the guilds in their defiance of the law sought only after their own "gloire." Also, inasmuch as they were represented in the town government and thus in the highest town court, they were acting in their own case against him. Here he was entering on dangerous ground, for if the guild-influenced town government indeed constituted "the authorities" with the right to establish legitimacy, then his case was lost. But locally it was lost anyway, and his appeal to the bishop invited the episcopal government to assert that they, not the Town Council, were "the authorities" in Hildesheim. The bishopric demanded that the Council issue formal judgment; but the Council, caught between state on one side and guilds on the other, found a temporary way out in a request for an opinion from the faculty of law at the University of Halle: Was the requirement of four legitimate grandparents legal? Was Helmsen legitimate (as book law said) or not (as the Hildesheimer said)? The Halle professors decided for Flegel and against the guilds, and the Council announced that decision. The smiths thereupon countered with the argument that the Halle faculty was not learned in Hildesheim local law and circumstance: community law breaks book law. Flegel was not reinstated nor his wife recognized. In 1747, five years after his marriage, he asked the Council to enforce the Halle decision; the Council issued the order, but nothing else happened. The Council then urged all concerned to try "good will" as a means to solution, and still nothing happened; but finally the bishopric ordered enforcement within two weeks. The Council summoned a meeting of the guild to admit Flegel, fearing military intervention by the bishop, but the hall remained empty; not a single master tinsmith appeared. Finally the Council ordered the guild to readmit Flegel and acknowledge the validity of his marriage lest episcopal soldiers and bureaucrats put an end to the privileges and autonomies of Hildesheim. The guild officers all resigned, and then there was nobody for the law to talk to.

Probably that is enough about the tinsmith Flegel. Eventually he was formally readmitted and his marriage registered, but that did not settle the case; after dragging on for several more years it disappeared into the episcopal courts. It is safe to say that Flegel never found a peaceable life in Hildesheim, for he had defied the procedures upon which community peace was founded. I cannot tell how he supported himself and his wife during the years of litigation and after, but it would fit the shape of the story if the answer has to do with the prospective father-in-law, with his belatedly acquired legitimacy, and his tainted daughter in need of a husband: money and political connections through Helmsen with the state may have helped evoke Flegel's tender emotions and his fellow guildsmen's righteousness. Defense of their honor against incursions like Flegel's was nothing new to the citizen-guildsmen of Hildesheim: they had defended it before against a master shoemaker who wanted to marry a piper's daughter, against a tailor who turned out to have a wet nurse for a mother, and against a smith who tried to register a miller's daughter as his wife. The social prudery and political stubbornness of the Hildesheim guilds were part of the character of every hometown community, and a role of guild organization was to lock those characteristics institutionally into the community as a whole. "For their functions," wrote Wolfram Fischer, "extended far beyond the economic, and their legal status placed them as integrating constituents of the political and social order of the old Empire. Only when we start with the social location of the guild and bring all its functions into consideration do we see the true role of the economic in the guild system." That "social location" was the home town; only there—not in the city and surely not the countryside—could the guilds assume so broad a role and still remain basically economic institutions. Only in the context of the home town is it comprehensible how the time of the notorious "decay" of the early modern German trades guilds should have been the period probably of their greatest power to impress their values and goals upon the society of which they were components.

To begin to describe them it is useful to separate out the several ways in which the hometown guilds entered into community life: economic regulation, political organization and representation, and guardianship of social or domestic standards. Each of these was a leg of the tripod upon which the influence of the guild relied. It is never easy to say in the event which aspect of guild life is at issue, for the guild readily introduced them all, and interchangeably to suit the case. Did the tinsmiths seize upon the chance to expel Flegel for economic reasons, because they feared competition from him? It is easy to suspect so, but the record does not show it. On the other hand there are instances enough where economic arguments—the overfilling of a trade, or the inability of a prospective master to support himself, for example—were used to exclude a candidate or prevent a marriage distasteful for quite other reasons. Or was Flegel's exclusion a political exercise? Almost surely it was in part, and if so then the nature of the case caused a political issue to be argued on grounds of domestic morality. The nineteenth century will be a better context for trying to distinguish motives. Here the linking of functions is the important thing to see. As occupational groupings within the community—of butchers, shoemakers, carpenters, and the rest—guilds supervised the recruitment, training, and allocation of individual citizens into the community's economy, and their economic character placed its stamp upon hometown morality and the nature of citizenship itself. As primary political organizers of the citizenry (in Rottweil the *Zünfte* with their component economic *Innungen*), they bore political and civic factors into economic practice and moral standards. And finally as moral and social watchdogs they saw to the quality of the citizenry— the *Ehre*, the honor, of the hometown workman and Bürger.

Still in the exercise of all these linked functions they worked as economic media; their special influence on the community and its membership rested ultimately on that role. That set the forms and the procedures whereby they carried out the rest, and shaped the mirror they held up to the whole community.

## The Guild Economy

The hometown guild artisan ordinarily sold his own products on the same premises where he produced them; or he performed skilled services within the specifically defined limits of the community. The customs and statutes that governed his training and regulated his activities were quite similar from one place to another, and based roughly on the same principles for each of the hometown trades, although there was wide variety in incidental customs and terminology. Craft guild rules which assumed a local but diversified economy set him apart from the merchant guildsmen of the cities (although some small towns had retailers' [*Krämer*] guilds entitled to sell certain imported goods locally), and set him apart also from the state-licensed or unorganized rural artisan. The rules were usually set down in written articles, statutes or charters prepared by each guild and confirmed or tolerated by some authority, much as the statutes of the towns themselves; and here too official confirmation had that troublesome effect of giving public force to private agreement, and custom had a local validity that was legally indistinct. The territorial government might itself confirm the statute, or even issue one on a conventional pattern; but usually confirmation came at the instance of the guild from the local magistracy or a local court. The guild's formal authority rested on that confirmed or acknowledged statute, which outlined its training program, the regulations governing the exercise of the trade, its powers to elect and to limit membership, the specific economic activity over which guild members held local monopoly (the *Zunftzwang*), and the geographical area (the *Bannmeile*) within which the monopoly prevailed. Sometimes an analytical distinction can be made between the guild's function as a training apparatus and as a corporate representative of an economic interest. But the distinction is formal only; within the community, rules to implement training programs were used to serve the economic and familial interests of the guildsmen, by holding down membership and excluding outsiders; conversely the economic interests of the trade were subject to pressure upon the guildsmen as members of the community to see to the useful education and social incorporation of the citizenry. Training and economic interest united in the critical decision of whether or not to admit a new master, and both were absorbed into the broader role of the guild within hometown society.

Guild statutes often set forth rules of guild life in remarkable detail, although of course much guild activity took place informally and unrecorded—which is not the same as to say quietly, by any means—and in conjunction with the cousins and brothers on the town councils and in the other trades. In the countryside, in professionally governed or mercantile cities like Hamburg and Nürnberg, and in the Prussian centralized country, incorporated craft guilds either did not exist or their structure was used as the channel for government regulation of the economy. But craft guilds within the hometown communities could not be reached by that kind of legislation or control because the civic community of uncles and brothers lay between, and because the guilds themselves were part of the communal system of authority.

A guild's affairs were administered by a collegial body of from two to four Overmasters . . . chosen by a process incorporating both the will of the membership and the choice of the civic authorities: some procedure along the whole spectrum running from direct appointment by the authorities to free election by a majority of guild masters. Where guild members elected their members independently, a member of the civic government (ordinarily a town councilor) was given the responsibility of overseeing a certain number of guilds and representing them to the government; and this overseer-patron, like the officers elected by the guildsmen themselves, was regularly paid by the guild and received certain irregular perquisites as well. The Overmasters decided internal conflicts, spelled out rules, levied fines and imposed minor punishments, administered guild finances and properties, saw to the inspection of masterworks prepared by candidates for mastership (though this might be done by a specially appointed inspector), and generally represented the interests of the trade, within the community and to the outside if need be. A guild court composed or dominated by these officials could expel any member who did not accept its decisions, and thus foreclose his practice of the trade; and frequently such a court punished members for civil or criminal misdeeds like theft or adultery, on the grounds (if anybody asked) that the transgression had brought the trade into disrepute, so that the trade must punish the offender to clear its name: that brought the case properly within guild jurisdiction.

The Overmasters were custodians of the Guild Chest, the *Lade*, a kind of ark of the guild covenant symbolizing the guild's corporate authority and autonomy, repository of its official documents and secrets, ceremonially opened on the occasion of meetings of the membership. Plenary meetings *(Morgensprachen)* were supposed to be held regularly—quarterly as a rule—but extraordinary meetings might be called to consider special problems, like a serious infraction of the rules by one of the members or some action by the authorities or by another trade that threatened the interests of the guild. A list of characteristic sources of guild income shows some of their activities:

1. periodic small fees paid like taxes by every master or widow actively in business;
2. interest on guild funds invested;
3. *Meistergeld*, the regular entry fees levied on new masters;
4. registration fees from apprentices;
5. buying-in fees (*Einkaufgeld*), either from accepted immigrating masters, or else in lieu of the masterwork or some other formal evidence of training; similarly
6. payments in lieu of the wanderyears;
7. fines levied on members for minor infractions.

Important guild expenditures included:

1. interest on loans taken out in the name of the guild;
2. salaries of guild officals and patrons;
3. food and drink for meetings;
4. subsistence money or "gifts" rendered to journeymen passing through town in search of work;
5. legal expenses;
6. relief to poor members for illness or burial, including the burial of poor or foreign journeymen;
7. relief to the bereaved families of members.

The several aspects of guild life converged on the master's estate, as citizen, head of household, and independent craftsman. The process of selection and induction began with apprenticeship. Active masters were expected to undertake the training of the sons of fellow townsmen as apprentices; apprentices were required to be Christians of honorable estate and parentage. After a trial period of a few weeks in a master's shop, petition was made to the Overmasters for formal registration of the apprentice with the guild; if his birth was properly certified and his other credentials met conditions set by the guild, he was admitted upon payment of a registration fee *(Einschreibegeld)* to the guild and a training fee *(Lehrgeld)* to the master. The registration fee was set by guild custom or statute; the training fee might be set by the statute or negotiated between the master and the parents of the apprentice. The apprentice was bound to serve the master loyally for a stated period, some three or four years, during which time the master for his part was obliged to give the apprentice real training and practice in the trade—not just use him as an errand boy—and a decent place in his domestic establishment. Now: often the sons of masters within the guild were forgiven the fees, or paid reduced fees, or were excused from apprenticeship altogether, or signed in and out on the same day without the regular period of training. The grounds were (again if anybody inquired) that a boy already knew what went on in his father's trade as well as an ordinary apprentice from another trade was expected to learn it; but it amounted to group favoritism and encouraged inbreeding within the trades. State laws frequently denounced the practice; so did the imperial edict of 1731; but enforcement necessarily was in the hands of local magistracies and guilds.

When the apprenticeship was done the young man paid another round of fees, usually underwent some convivial hazing, and thus was promoted to journeyman. The journeyman was presumed to have learned the basic skills of his trade, but he was not yet ready to carry it on independently. First he was to go on a round of travels, working at a wage for other masters in other places, and getting the behavior of late adolescence out of his system, away from home but still free of the responsibilities and encumbrances of a domestic establishment of his own. His training and good reputation were certified by the guild in which he had served his apprenticeship, so that the guild, its reputation at stake, was careful with the certification; similarly the journeyman relied on the good name of his home guild (or absence of a bad name) for his acceptance abroad. His written certification for public display might, especially if his home guild claimed special virtues, be supplemented by some special, secret, visual or oral sign, to commend him to those guilds abroad that would recognize the sign.

When a journeyman arrived at a new town he went to the journeymen's hostel sponsored by his trade there, and applied to the host, the *Herbergsvater* appointed by the guild, for work. The host directed him to a local master looking for help if there was one; if no work could be found within a stipulated short period, probably no more than a day and a night, the journeyman was sent on his way with the help of a small grant from the guild treasury, the gift or *Zehrpfennig*. If he stayed in town without work he was treated as a vagrant, for that is what he was; strange unemployed journeymen meant beggars and thieves to the home town.

There at the hostel he ordinarily lived, while he was locally employed; and his papers were deposited in the guild chest controlled by the Overmasters. Only a master or a master's widow in his learned trade could legitimately employ him: if he valued his prospects as master and Bürger he would not enter the service of a noble, nor of the state, nor work at a factory, nor go as a soldier or a servant. After a given minimum term of employment in one place the journeyman might leave to resume his wandering, or be dismissed by his employer, when proper notice was given and the piece he was working on was finished; sometimes there were customary appointed calendar times: for example quarterly for the tailors, after Easter, Midsummer, Michaelmas in September, and Christmas; and for shoemakers, Midsummer and Christmas. His papers were endorsed by the local guild to show that he had worked there, and how he had behaved. If a journeyman ran off he left his credentials behind him in the guild chest, and he needed them, with endorsements, for acceptance into a respectable trade in any respectable place.

Life at the hostel was often organized on the pattern of the masters' guild, with overjourneymen, meetings, and a chest; there were fines, and mutual assistance in case of misfortune. But the journeymen's organizations, with their transient membership of dependent labor, never attained the local influence nor the local interest of the guild of the masters; their interests and influence were rather related to their transience, and differences that arose between them and the masters resulted from their transient status—the fact that they would soon be moving on and would need acceptance elsewhere—far more commonly than from conflicts over wages or working conditions. They were moreover unmarried, and were not made citizens.

The term of travel varied in length from place to place and from trade to trade, and the rules were shot through besides with dispensations for fees, or for familial reasons, or both together: favoritism for sons, or special arrangements for journeymen who married the widows or orphan daughters of local masters. But two or more years of attested wandering was a customary condition for application for mastership. Far and away the best place for a journeyman to apply for mastership —barring a palatable widow or orphan—was in his home town, so there he usually returned when his wanderyears were done. His application was filed with the Overmasters of the guild to which he sought entry, and after their evaluation it was laid before the assembled masters and usually before the civil authorities as well. He had to provide certification of apprentice training that the local masters would accept, proof of his travels to proper places and of proper behavior when he was there, and of course above all he had again to prove legitimate ancestry. All of these conditions were more easily met by a local boy, unless there was something wrong with him, than by an outsider.

The examination of all these qualifications offered plenty of opportunities to exclude the candidate if the masters so chose, and if they could exclude him without offending colleagues, relatives, neighbors, and customers. Yet another hurdle was the masterwork, an exhibition of the candidate's skill prepared in the place where he applied. What the masterwork should be was assigned by local guild statute, by custom, or by the guild *ad hoc* when it authorized the candidate to make and submit it. It was easy to assign a difficult piece of work or an expensive one, and then if need be still to reject it in the name of the guild's high standards: where, young man, did you learn to make things *that* way? If the trade was overfilled—limits on membership might be set by guild statute, by town or even state ordinance, or by the judgment of the guildsmen—then the candidate might be rejected on that ground, or told to wait; and there was no guarantee that he might not later be bypassed for a more recent candidate who found greater favor. Another economic condition was that the candidate must prove he had the resources to establish his shop and assume the burdens of citizen and family head, some combination of tools and cash, perhaps; and often he was obliged to commit himself to the community by building or buying a house. Guilds commonly denied mastership to any bachelor, a practice that not only enjoined domestic commitment but helped the marital prospects of guild widow and orphan, not to mention unplaced daughters of the community as a whole: thus marriage ordinarily coincided with admission to mastership. The property requirement was applied most stringently upon outsiders; citizens' sons with presumptive claim on citizenship and a local economic base in the family trade had a far easier time of it. The same was true of the waiting period, the *Muthjahren* or *Sitzjahren*, that lay between the fully trained journeyman's application for mastership and the decision whether or not to accept him. Its main purpose was to give guildsmen and citizens a chance to look him over, and it was mainly strangers that were subjected to the waiting period, not those whose backgrounds and propects were known.

The stranger upon whom these conditions were imposed was a stranger no more by the time he had fulfilled them all; proof of family background and domestic intent, locally produced masterwork, material resources in the town and a place in its economy, and time to learn about the community and for the community to learn about him. Familiarity and community acceptance was the real purpose of it all. That is why waiving the rules for local boys of respectable family made perfect sense to the hometownsmen, though to anyone from outside the hometown, to anyone who thought of guilds purely as economic instruments, the communal working of the system smelled— and still does—of corruption, decadence, and economic malfunction.

The new master now shared in the local guild monopoly and agreed to abide by its rules. The guild monopoly made good economic sense within the community insofar as it maintained an appropriate balance and relation in and among the trades without exposing any citizen to ruinous competition, and assured that only skilled and responsible practitioners would pursue each of them. It was, to be sure, a system of mutual defense by guildsmen-citizens. But any guild that showed itself so restrictive as seriously to undersupply the local economy (and the local economy is in question here, no more), or to exclude citizens' sons without economic justification, incurred community pressure to ease entries into the trade, and it invited breaches of its monopoly which the community and its authorities would consider justified. If a trade grew very rich, it would attract sons of influential families who could not easily be excluded by numerical limitations. The hometown guild monopolies were enforcements of the rules whereby the community kept its soundness and autonomy, directed first of all against outsiders but also against any citizen who failed to go along with the rules. . . .

## Guild Moralism and the Integrated Personality

The extremes and the eccentricities of guild moralism remain puzzling after all reasonable explanations have been used up, and may be, like some kinds of eccentric personal behavior, a signal of the matter's importance. One explanation is that the notion of honorable status, of *Ehrbarkeit*, with which they were intensely concerned, was so broad and vague a slogan that it provided no reasonable or functional limits. *Ehrbarkeit* (often *Redlichkeit* or decency) could not be clearly defined or objectively ascertained, like wealth, skill, or performance; it was something sensed as it was displayed and received within a community of whom all shared the same standards. Outsiders could detect wealth or skill, and there were laws to define civil crime; but neither could tell about moral honor, not all of it. Its imprecise character led the guildsmen into absurdities of prurience and persecution when they tried to judge and act upon it. There was no check on their eagerness to show their own morality by the severity with which they judged others.

The main preoccupation with legitimacy of birth, which extended by easy stages into questions of sexual behavior and social background, had a reasonable foundation in the domestic character of community and economy: the importance of knowing who somebody was, and the soundess of his family circumstances. The guild encompassed the citizen-master's life, not just his occupation. His family was part of his occupation and his guild; his widow and his orphans were cared for by it and his sons were specially privileged within it. But legitimacy was not only nor even mainly a matter of inheritance rights; there were plenty of adequate laws to handle those. *Ehrbarkeit* meant domestic, civic, and economic orderliness and these were undermined by the promiscuity and irresponsibility implied by illegitimate birth. Legitimate childbirth resulted from sober and responsible intention to have a child, whose conception bore the community's sanction; illegitimacy implied the contrary. The trouble with Flegel's father-in-law, according to the Hildesheim tinsmiths, was that he was not *echt und recht erzielt,* not "truly and rightly begot" in the sense of "intended." Not to have been intended was a fact presumed to have effect on Helmsen's attitude and behavior in the world, whatever the bishop said; and that would influence his daughter too. So much seems clear enough in guildsmen's attitude toward legitimacy of birth, and there is a hint besides that along with the danger of irresponsible laxity, illegitimacy might imply an equally unappropriate and distasteful aggressiveness.

It might be argued that moral sanctions were directed less against loose sexual behavior as such than at its social consequences: the foisting upon the community of persons with uncertain origins and uncertain qualifications for membership. The hometownsman's pride was closely involved in the guild's quest for purity. More mobile elements of German society were held by hometownsmen to be sexually and maritally promiscuous, so that sexual and marital purity were a caste mark that guildsmen-citizens employed to set themselves apart. It was important to be different from lower elements especially, from the rooting peasantry with its servile origins and style. Then there were the merchants and peddlers, traveling salemen of their day, trying like cuckoos to pass off their bastards into the artisanry; and loose-living aristocrats had to be watched for that too. The guilds took special pains to be sure no artisan married a fallen woman for a price, apparently a frequent source of moral infection and hard to distinguish from more normal premarital pregnancies: the 1731 edict mentioned the problem of "marriage of a female person made pregnant when unmarried by yet another person."

No doubt the guilds used ostensibly moral grounds to exclude persons held undesirable for reasons not strictly moral—not directly concerned with sex or marriage, that is, but exclusion for economic or civic reasons. In such cases the search for moral grounds, with their special psychological force and appeal, led to some of the oddities and extremes. Put moralism for the sake of exclusion together with sexual purity as the hometownsman's mark of caste, and guild moralism becomes a specific instrument for excluding unwanted social elements from the community, and as such its use was stretched to the borders of credibility. It helped screen out unwanted outsiders, regardless of social estate, because it was so much harder for them than for natives to prove honorable family background. In other moral questions too, not only did the outsider have little evidence to offer for himself, his very arrival at the gates made him suspect of having become *persona non grata* elsewhere, and chances are he had. Why hadn't he applied to his own home town, where people knew him? It was easier for such a man to rove countryside and city than it was to enter the hometown as a Bürger.

The taint of illegitimacy lasted for generations; the same was true of other dishonorable estates. The list of dishonorable occupations coheres only in the moral sense of the hometown guildsmen who made it; it is almost without limit because each guild and each place had to show itself more discriminating than the rest, and no one could dissent from any instance without jeop-

ardizing his own honor. Hangmen first of all: the usual taboo of
the executioner, but hometown hangmen got a lot of other
disgraceful work as well: clearing carrion, burying rotten fish.
Even the 1731 edict did not dare call the sons of hangmen
honorable. Skinners worked with dead bodies too, and the word
*Schinder* was sometimes used to mean both hangman and skin-
ner. The line between what skinners did with carcasses and
what butchers and tanners did with meat and hides was elabo-
rately guarded, but not well enough to keep the tanners free of
taint. Barbers and surgeons worked with wounds, a disgusting
and servile business. So did bathers, and doubtless besides there
were promiscuous goings-on at the baths. The lofts of mills were
morally suspect too, and millers swindling middlemen and
speculators to boot. Shepherds were contemptible everywhere.
What kind of a man would be a shepherd? They skinned dead
sheep (the flayed Lamb of God prominent in religious symbol-
ism of the time may have enhanced that feature), and the same
stories about a shepherd's relations with his sheep seem to have
been told that I heard in New England as a boy. The weaving
of linen was another primitive occupation, and like shepherd-
ing had suspect rural overtones and connections. Musicians and
players moved from place to place, like itinerant peddlers and
beggars. And officials of the state: their sons were adjudged
dishonorable by the guildsmen, should they ever think of entering a hometown trade. It was a mark of dishonor to have
worked as a peasant, or for a noble, or in a factory, a *Fabrik*. It
was a sign of failure and dishonor for a master to work in a
factory, wrote Sieber; if he took work there it was because,
despite his failure, his master's status kept him from being employed like a journeyman by another master. As for journeymen
who worked in factories: what kind of training was to be had in
a place where things were made in large anonymous numbers
and sold to customers the maker did not know? Not the right
kind of preparation for the hometown trades.

Guild morality equated the outsider with dishonor; those two

factors of repulsion multiplied together to produce guild moralism's intensity and its righteousness. It is important to note
here that guilds, economic institutions, bore this spirit in the
hometown community. The fervid moral preoccupation of the
guilds, like their social and economic restrictiveness, seems
mainly to have developed in the seventeenth and eighteenth
centuries. There had been dishonorable occupations for long
before that (mainly the more reasonable ones), but little sign
that moral fervor had been an important part of guild life. It was
a part of the multiplication of their role beyond the custody of
economic standard and training. That role was multiplied by
the maintenance of social continuity and stability, and that by
the guardianship of civic standards, and finally all united into
morality in the sense of personal justification, of the kind tradi-
tionally in the hands of religious institutions—*moral* morality,
the morality of conscience. The curious stock expression, "The
guilds must be as pure, as if they had been gathered together
by doves," seems to have originated in the seventeenth century. It may be that in the background of the early modern
German craft guild's moral guardianship was the weakening
and dispersal of religious institutions after the wars of religion:
institutions perhaps with more experience and discrimination
in moral questions than the home town. Civic authority had
taken up moral custody first: not only state laws but seventeenth-century town statutes were full of religious and moral
exhortations. But these had nearly disappeared by the mid-
eighteenth century. And when the guild assumed the moral
role, it adapted moral questions, unsurprisingly, to its economic
structure and interests and to its place in the civic community.
The guild, first habitat of the hometown Bürger, blended economic and civic and personal standards together into the moral
quality of honor, in such a way that a man's personal morals—
and his ancestors'—determined his economic competence and
his civic rights; at the same time economic competence was
prerequisite for civic and moral acceptance; and at the same

time responsible civic membership was requisite for economic rights and personal justification. Such a combination might be called bourgeois morality, but like the political standards mentioned before it was the morality of the hometownsman, not the mobile and sophisticated high bourgeois. Hometownsmen did not have the multiple standards and compartmentalized lives that so many modern moral and social critics deplore: one set of standards for church on Sunday, another for relations with friends, another for business relations. They were whole men, integrated personalities, caught like so many flies in a three-dimensional web of community.

The totality of the web made the moralism with which the hometownsman defended his economic interests, and the righteousness he brought to his politics; it provided the aura of depravity and evil he attributed to rivals and strangers. The guilds in their connective functions—between citizen and community, and among compartments of life we incline to treat separately—were vital institutions of communal defense and also main determiners of what it was that would be defended, and against whom. Guildsmen were the wall and the web incarnate. The hometown community rested on the guild economy, and fell only when the guild economy was overwhelmed.

# 3

# THE WHEELWRIGHT'S SHOP

## George Sturt

It was as a young schoolteacher that George Sturt decided in 1884 to enter the wheelwright business of his ailing father. A short time after the father died, leaving the bookish Sturt in charge of a substantial enterprise in the village of Farnham (Surrey), which employed eight men and produced not just wheels but entire farm wagons. For several years thereafter Sturt struggled desperately to learn the trade so as to carry on the firm. This chronicle, which he wrote in 1923 after definite paralysis had ended his active life, tells the story of a young intellectual's initiation into craftwork. As a quick-witted, literate observer who came from outside to end up knowing the trade intimately, Sturt provides an unusual perspective on the world of work of the craftsman. This is how it was in the old craft shop, in part, for Sturt confesses himself to have been at the beginning heavily influenced by John Ruskin's romantic visions of handwork. In retrospect Sturt attempted to place his own infatuation with craftwork in perspective, yet thick layers of nostalgia remain in the account. Separating out the ideological celebration of the craft system, the youthful memories of a declining elderly man, and the historic reality of life in the small shop, is a difficult evidential problem in this variety of history.

SOURCE: George Sturt, *The Wheelwright's Shop* (New York: Cambridge University Press paperback edition 1963), pp. 17–24, 53–61, 83–87, 197–203. Reprinted with permission of the Cambridge University Press. Footnotes omitted.

To say that the business I started into in 1884 was old-fashioned is to understate the case: it was a "folk" industry, carried
on in a "folk" method. And circumstances made it perhaps
more intensely so to me than it need have been. My father
might just possibly, though I don't think he would, have shown
me more modern aspects of it; but within my first month he
took ill of the illness he died of five months later. Consequently
I was left to pick up the business as best I could from "the men."
There were never any "hands" with us. Eight skilled workmen
or apprentices, eight friends of the family, put me up to all they
could: and since some of them had been born and trained in
little old country shops, while this of my father's was not much
better, the lore I got from them was of the country through and
through.

The objects of the work too were provincial. There was no
looking far afield for customers. Farmers rarely more than five
miles away; millers, brewers, a local grocer or builder or timber-
merchant or hop-grower—for such and no others did the ancient shop still cater, as it had done for nearly two centuries.
And so we got curiously intimate with the peculiar needs of the
neighbourhood. In farm-waggon or dung-cart, barley-roller,
plough, water-barrel, or what not, the dimensions we chose, the
curves we followed (and almost every piece of timber was
curved) were imposed upon us by the nature of the soil in this
or that farm, the gradient of this or that hill, the temper of this
or that customer or his choice perhaps in horseflesh. The carters
told us their needs. To satisfy the carter, we gave another half-
inch of curve to the waggon-bottom, altered the hooks for har-
ness on the shafts, hung the water-barrel an inch nearer to the
horse or an inch farther away, according to requirements.

One important point, which it's true was not always important (for hard roads, for instance) but was sometimes very important indeed, was to make the wheels of waggon or dung-cart

"take the routs," as we said. A variant of this was to get the wheels of a waggon to "follow," the hind wheels cutting the same ruts as the front. One inch of variation was allowed, no more. The track of new dung-cart or waggon might measure 5 ft. 10½ ins. or 5 ft. 11½ ins. "over," that is, from outside to outside. A miry lane at a farm revealed to me the importance of keeping to this measurement. Two parallel ruts went all down the lane, deep as the hub of a cart wheel. Many carts, for many years perhaps, had followed there; and plainly the lane would be impassable for any cart or waggon with wheels too wide asunder or too narrow. So, the wheel-spaces were standardised.

This was but one of the endless details the complete wheelwright had to know all about. For the complete wheelwright, acquiring skill of eyes and hands to make a wheel, was good enough workman then for the job of building a waggon throughout and painting it too; and all this was expected of him. There was a tale (of another shop than mine) of an aged man who, having built and painted a waggon, set about "writing" (lettering) the owner's name and address on the small name-board fixed to the off front side. He managed all right until he came to the address, "Swafham" or "Swayle," but this word puzzled him. He scratched his head, at last had to own himself baffled; and appealed to his mate. "Let's see, Gearge," he said, "blest if I ain't forgot how you makes a Sway!"

Gearge showed him.

Truly there were mysteries enough, without the mystery of "writing," for an unlettered man. Even the mixing and putting on of the paint called for experience. The first two coats, of Venetian-red for the underworks and shafts and "lid colour" (lead colour) for the "body," prepared the way for the putty, which couldn't be "knocked-up" by instinct; and then came the last coat, of red-lead for the wheels and Prussian-blue for the body, to make all look smart and showy.

Not any of this could be left wholly to an apprentice. Apprentices, after a year or two, might be equal to making and painting a wheelbarrow. But it was a painful process with them learning the whole trade. Seven years was thought not too long. After seven years, a young man, newly "out of his time" was held likely to pick up more of his craft in the next twelve months than he had dreamt of before. By then too he should have won the skill that came from wounds. For it was a saying of my grandfather's that nobody would learn to make a wheel without chopping his knee half-a-dozen times.

There was nothing for it but practice and experience of every difficulty. Reasoned science for us did not exist. "Theirs not to reason why." What we had to do was to live up to the local wisdom of our kind; to follow the customs, and work to the measurements, which had been tested and corrected long before our time in every village shop all across the country. A wheelwright's brain had to fit itself to this by dint of growing into it, just as his back had to fit into the supplenesses needed on the saw-pit, or his hands into the movements that would plane a felloe "true out o' wind." Science? Our two-foot rules took us no nearer to exactness than the sixteenth of an inch: we used to make or adjust special gauges for the nicer work; but very soon a stage was reached when eye and hand were left to their own cleverness, with no guide to help them. So the work was more of an art—a very fascinating art—than a science; and in this art, as I say, the brain had its share. A good wheelwright knew by art but not by reasoning the proportion to keep between spokes and felloes; and so too a good smith knew how tight a two-and-a-half inch tyre should be made for a five-foot wheel and how tight for a four-foot, and so on. He felt it, in his bones. It was a perception with him. But there was no science in it; no reasoning. Every detail stood by itself, and had to be learnt either by trial and error or by tradition.

This was the case with all dimensions. I knew how to "line out" a pair of shafts on a plank, and had in fact lined and helped saw on the saw-pit hundreds of them, years before I understood, thinking it over, why this method came right. So too it was years before I understood why a cart wheel needed a certain convexity although I had seen wheels fall to pieces for want of it. It was a detail most carefully attended to by the men in my shop; but I think none of them, any more than myself, could have explained why it had to be so.

Some things I never learnt at all, they being all but obsolete even in that primitive shop. To say nothing of square-tongued wheels—a mystery I still think of with some awe—there was the placing of the "tines" in a wooden harrow that remained an unknown secret to me. The opportunities of investigating it had been too few when cast-iron harrows, ready-made, banished the whole subject from our attention. I just learnt how the harrow was put together to be hauled over the field by one corner; but the trick of mortising the teeth—the "tines"—into it so that no two cut the same track—this was known to one elderly man but never to me. The same man also failed to teach me how to "line out" a wooden axle. Indeed, he forgot it himself at last. So it happened that when an ancient dung-cart arrived, needing a wooden axle for its still serviceable wheels, nobody was quite sure how to mark out the axle on the bone-hard bit of beech that was found for it. It was then that my rather useless schooling came in handy for once. With a little geometry I was able to pencil out on the beech the outlines of an axle to serve (in its clumsier dimensions) the better-known purposes of iron. Yet I have no doubt that the elderly wheelwright's tradition would have been better, if only he could have remembered it.

## Buying

One aspect of the death of Old England and of the replacement of the more primitive nation by an "organised" modern state was brought out forcibly and very disagreeably by the War against Germany [1914–1918]. It was not only that one saw the beautiful fir-woods going down, though that was bad. The trees, cut into lengths, stripped of their bark and stacked in piles, gave to many an erst secluded hill-side a staring publicity. This or that quiet place, the home of peace, was turned into a ghastly battle-field, with the naked and maimed corpses of trees lying about. Bad enough, all this was. Still, trees might grow again; the hollows might recover their woodland privacy and peace for other generations to enjoy. But what would never be recovered, because in fact War had found it already all but dead, was the earlier English understanding of timber, the local knowledge of it, the patriarchal traditions of handling it. Of old there had been a close relationship between the tree-clad countryside and the English who dwelt there. But now, the affection and the reverence bred of this—for it had been with something near to reverence that a true provincial beheld his native trees—was all but gone. A sort of greedy prostitution desecrated the ancient woods. All round me I saw and heard of things being done with a light heart that had always seemed to me wicked—things as painful to my sympathies as harnessing a carriage-horse to a heavy dray, or as pulling down a cathedral to get building-stone. I resented it; resented seeing the fair timber callously felled at the wrong time of year, cut up too soon, not "seasoned" at all. Perhaps the German sin had made all this imperative; yet it was none the less hateful. Not as waste only was it hateful: it was an outrage on the wisdom of our forefathers—a wanton insult put upon Old England, in her woods and forests.

The new needs were so different from the old. What had been prized once was prized no more. The newer vehicles, motor drawn, were not expected to last longer than eight or ten years at the most; five years, oftener, found them obsolete, and therefore durability was hardly considered in the timber used for their construction. But it was otherwise in the earlier time, in the old-fashioned wheelwright's shop. Any piece of work had to last for years. Fashion, or invention, didn't affect it. So it was held a shame to have to do work twice over because the original material had been faulty; and I have known old-fashioned workmen refuse to use likely-looking timber because they held it to be unfit for the job.

And they knew. The skilled workman was the final judge. Under the plane (it is little used now) or under the axe (it is all but obsolete) timber disclosed qualities hardly to be found otherwise. My own eyes know because my own hands have felt, but I cannot teach an outsider, the difference between ash that is "tough as whipcord," and ash that is "frow as a carrot," or "doaty," or "biscuity." In oak, in beech, these differences are equally plain, yet only to those who have been initiated by practical work. These know how "green timber" (that is, timber with some sap left in it, imperfectly "seasoned") does not look like properly dried timber, after planing. With axe or chisel or draw-shave they learn to distinguish between the heart of a plank and the "sap." And again, after years of attention, but nohow else, timber-users can tell what "shakes" are good and what bad. For not all shakes, all natural splits, in seasoned timber are injurious. On the contrary it was an axiom in my shop that good timber in drying was bound to "open" (care had to be taken to prevent it from opening too far) and that timber must be bad, must have lost all its youthful toughness, if the process of drying developed no shakes in it. . . .

## Kindly Feeling

I should soon have been bankrupt in business in 1884 if the public temper then had been like it is now—grasping, hustling, competitive. But then no competitor seems to have tried to hurt me. To the best of my remembrance people took a sort of benevolent interest in my doings, put no difficulties in my way, were slow to take advantage of my ignorance. Nobody asked for an estimate—indeed there was a fixed price for all the new work that was done. The only chance for me to make more profit would have been by lowering the quality of the output; and this the temper of the men made out of the question. But of profits I understood nothing. My great difficulty was to find out the customary price. The men didn't know. I worked out long lists of prices from the old ledgers, as far as I could understand their technical terms.

Commerical travellers treated me well—Sanders from Auster & Co., Bryant from Simpson's, Dyball from Noble & Hoare. The last-named, I remember, fearing that I was in danger of over-stocking, could hardly be persuaded to book an order for four gallons of varnish, when he was expecting it to be for only two gallons. It was not until customers had learnt to be shy of my book-learned ignorance, my simplicity, my Ruskinian absurdities, that they began to ask for estimates, or to send their work elsewhere.

The steadiness of the men was doubtless what saved me from ruin. Through them I felt the weight of the traditional public attitude towards industry. They possibly (and properly) exaggerated the respect for good workmanship and material; and I cannot blame them if they slowed down in pace. Workmen even to-day do not understand what a difference this may make to an employer. The main thing after all (and the men in my shop were faithful to it) was to keep the business up to a high level, preserving the reputation my father and grandfather had won for it. To make it pay—that was not their affair. Certainly they taught me how to be economical, in "lining-out" the timber and so on; but the time came when I found it needful to curb their own extravagance, scheming all sorts of ways, for instance, to get three shafts out of a plank, where a too fastidious workman would have cut only two. It rarely happened the other way about, rarely happened that the condemnation of a piece of timber came from me; but it did happen, not infrequently, that a disgusted workman would refuse to use what I had supplied to him.

In this temper the shop, I feel sure, turned out good work. Especially the wheels which George Cook used to make were, I am bound to think, as good as any that had been built under the eyes of two experts like my father and his father. Cook, it is pretty sure, took his own time; but what a workman he was! There was another wheelwright in the shop whose wife used to take out garden produce in a little van: and when the van wanted new wheels, this man would not make them himself but asked that George Cook might make them. Truly, it was a liberal education to work under Cook's guidance. I never could get axe or plane or chisel sharp enough to satisfy him; but I never doubted, then or since, that his tiresome fastidiousness over tools and handiwork sprang from a knowledge as valid as any artist's. He knew, not by theory, but more delicately, in his eyes and fingers. Yet there were others almost his match—men who could make the wheels, and saw out on the saw-pit the other timbers for a dung-cart, and build the cart and paint it— preparing the paint first; or, if need be, help the blacksmith tyring the wheels. And two things are notable about these men. Of the first, indeed, I have already given some hint: it is, that in them was stored all the local lore of what good wheelwright's work should be like. The century-old tradition was still vigorous in them. They knew each customer and his needs; understood his carters and his horses and the nature of his land; and finally took a pride in providing exactly what was wanted in every case. So, unawares, they lived as integral parts in the rural community of the English. Overworked and underpaid, they none the less enjoyed life, I am sure. They were friends, as only a craftsman can be, with timber and iron. The grain of the wood told secrets to them.

The other point is, that these men had a special bond of comfort in the regard they felt for my own family. This was of old standing. Consideration had been shown to them— a sort of human thoughtfulness—for very long. My grandfather, I heard more than once, wanting to arrange his wayzgoose [a family party] for Christmas, had been careful not to fix it for the same day as the wayzgoose at Mason's, the carpenter's, but to have it so that the sawyers, who worked for both firms, could attend both feasts. My father had been habitually considerate. "The men" sought his advice as if they were his trusting children. He and his brothers had all mastered the trade: they were looked up to as able workmen; they always chose the hardest work for themselves. It was my father who was furnaceman at "shoeing" (putting the iron tyres on the wheels); who sharpened the pit-saws, acted as "striker" to the smiths for special jobs, stacked the timber—never spared himself. Thanks largely to him a sort of devotion to the whole family had grown up in the shop, and in time was of incalculable help to me, all inexperienced. For some years I was called familiarly by my Christian name; and when at last it was more usual to hear myself called "the gov'ner," still something like affection followed me; not because I was an able workman (I had had no apprenticeship for that), but because I was heir to a tradition of friendly behaviour to "the men." Older than myself though most of them were, while all were abler, they seemed to me often like a lot of children—tiresome children sometimes. And still they came to me for help and advice, in their own small business difficulties.

## Hand-Work

There was no machinery, or at any rate there was no steam or other "power," in my father's shop in 1884. Everything had to be done by hand, though we had implements to serve ma-chine-uses in their feeble way. I myself have spent hours turn-ing the grindstone. It stood under a walnut tree; and in sunny weather there might have been worse jobs. Only, sometimes the grinding lasted too long—especially for a new tool, or for an axe. Cook was a terror in this respect. Time seemed no object with him; he must get his edge. And he had a word I used to wonder at. For when a new plane or chisel proved over-brittle, so that a nick chinked out of it and needed grinding wholly away, Cook used to look disapprovingly at the broken edge and mutter "Crips." What was that word? I never asked. Besides, Cook was too deaf. But after some years it dawned upon me that he had meant crisp.

Another implement to be turned with a handle was a drill, for drilling tyres for the blacksmiths. To put this round, under its horizontal crank, was harder work than turning the grindstone. The shaft of it went up through the ceiling to a loft, where a circular weight—a heavy iron wheel in fact—gave the pressure on the drill. Men took turns at drilling, for it was often a long job. I don't remember doing much of this; yet I well remember the battered old oil-tin, and the little narrow spoon, and the smell of the linseed oil, as we fed it to the drill to prevent over-heating.

More interesting—but I was never man enough to use it—was a lathe, for turning the hubs of waggon and cart wheels. I suspect it was too clumsy for smaller work. Whenever I think of this, shame flushes over me that I did not treasure up this ancient thing, when at last it was removed. My grandfather had made it—so I was told. Before his time the hubs or stocks of wheels had been merely rounded up with an axe in that shop, because there was no lathe there, or man who could use one. But my grandfather had introduced this improvement when he came to the shop as foreman; and there the lathe remained until my day. I had seen my father covered with the tiny chips from it (the floor of the "lathe-house" it stood in was a foot deep in such chips), and too late I realized that it was a curiosity in its way.

On a stout post from floor to ceiling was swung a large wheel —the hind wheel for a waggon—to serve for pulley. All round the rim of this slats were nailed, or perhaps screwed on. They stood up on both sides of the felloes [wooden sections of the rim of a wheel] so as to form a run or channel for the leather belting that was carried over the pulley-wheel, across to the stock to be turned. A big handle, which years of use had polished smooth and shiny, stood out from the spokes of this wheel, just within the rim. Gripping this handle two men (but it took two) could put the wheel round fast enough for the turner with his gouge. They supplied the needful "power." Thanks to them a fourteen-inch stock could be kept spinning in the lathe. And had I but realised it in time, near at hand was a most interesting proof of the advantages of this implement. For the stock of the waggon wheel—that very wheel now used for turning other stocks—had not itself been turned. It had only been rounded up very neatly with an axe, in the old-fashioned way. It puzzles me now how they could ever have built a wheel at all on so inexact a foundation.

But the want of machinery was most evident in the daily task of cutting up plank or board for other work, and of planing and mortising afterwards. We had neither band-saw nor circular saw. Most of the felloes were shaped out by adze and axe: the pieces for barrow-wheel felloes were clamped to a woodman's bench (for they were too short and small for an axe), and sawed out there by a boy with a frame-saw (I hated the job—it was at once lonely and laborious); the heavy boards were cut out (and edged up) with a hand-saw, being held down on the trestles with your knee (it was no joke to cut a set of one-inch elm boards —for a waggon-bottom—your arm knew about it); but all the timbers for framework of waggon or cart, or harrow or plough or wheelbarrow, were cut out by two men on a saw-pit.

From my childhood I had liked this saw-pit. It lay under a penthouse—just beyond the grindstone already mentioned; and in summer the walnut-tree over the grindstone sent a cool and dappled shadow down on the tiles of the saw-pit roof. The sill at the farther end was cumbered up with lengths of timber standing on end—timber "in cut," as we said, meaning that widths had been already cut off from it. But if you merely jumped across the saw-pit to the opposite side you were brought up short by a tier of plank stacked there to get the shelter of the roof. When this plank came to be moved (but that was not often) it disclosed tarred weather-boarding, closing in that side of the saw-pit penthouse from the public lane outside.

A short old piece of ladder enabled one to get down the five or six feet into the saw-pit. On either hand was brickwork—two bricks having been left out, each side, to hold an oil-cup, and wedges for the "saw-box" which clutched the bottom-end of the saw. But the "box" itself, and the little oily club for knocking it on, might be tossed down anywhere on to the layer of sawdust at the bottom. Sometimes a frog was hopping about in this sawdust, sometimes one saw a black beetle there. The sight of this quiet fauna gave me, as a child, a sense of great peace. The aged-looking brickwork—greyish pink and very dusty—helped the impression, and so did the planks stacked on the sill at the side. The daylight seemed to float in a sort of dusty ease amongst the planks and the sawdust, as if nothing noisier than a frog or a black beetle need be thought of there.

And there I found the same settled peace when, as a young man, at last I began to go down into the saw-pit to work. Certainly peace was beneficial; for sawing was hard work and often lasted a whole day—or more than that, if the timbers for a new waggon were to be sawed out. One got a queer glimpse of the top-sawyer, as one glanced up (with puckered eyelids) through the falling sawdust. Gradually the dust accumulated about one's feet, and eventually it had to be shovelled up into sacks. Being from dry timber, and mostly oak, it was useful for bacon-curing, and I used to sell it for that purpose at fourpence the sack.

Excepting that the timber was harder yet thinner (for it was dry plank instead of green round timber) and also that the work was far more varied—excepting for these reasons this pit-sawing I took part in was not very different from a professional sawyer's. I never had confidence enough, or muscle enough, to choose the top-sawyer's arduous post: I was only bottom-sawyer. And truly the work was hard enough there, though I sus-

pect I didn't do my share. I suspect so, judging by the frequency
of the top-sawyer's exhortations to "Chuck her up." (Pit-saws
were always feminine.) How was a man to chuck her up when
his back was one ache and all he could do for rest was to lean
his weight on the handles of the saw-box for the down-pull?
When the down-streaming sawdust caked on his sweaty arms
and face? And thirst too! After those parched hours I have
always felt that there were excuses for the notorious drunken-
ness of sawyers, who had not hours but years of this exhausting
drudgery to endure.

Not but there were compensations, at least for the bottom
man. He might not, indeed, quite go to sleep. He had to keep
the saw perpendicular, to watch "the cut" as best he could
through the ever-descending sawdust, and now and again he
halted (straightening his back) to carry out the blessed command from the top-sawyer to drive in a wedge or to "oil-up."
But with these exceptions the bottom-sawyer's lot was placid in
the extreme. The work was hard enough to prevent thought,
there was nothing to see beyond the brick walls of the saw-pit,
and the up-and-down sway of arms and body was frequent
enough and regular enough to induce a restful drowsiness.

Yet, fatiguing though it was, the work was full of interest—
for me, who owned the timber, and for the skilled man who was
going to work it up. We both were anxious to see how it looked
after sawing—if any knot or shake or rind-gall or other unsus-
pected flaw should make it necessary to condemn this or that
piece and to start again. On the other hand we were sometimes
rewarded by the sight of really beautiful "stuff"—beautiful, that
is to say, in the qualities only an expert could discern.

Of course before the sawing could begin we had taken much
pains to find the right timber and to mark it out. As I made a
practice of doing this for every job, whereby nothing was used
without my knowledge (it was my father's way), so my acquaint-
ance with the individual pieces (planks and "flitches," to say
nothing of spokes and felloes and hubs) became intimate and

exhaustive. I spent hours, often by myself, hunting for just the exact piece that would be wanted, perhaps, to-morrow. Or, was any man about to begin on new cart, or waggon, or wheelbarrow, he looked to me to find him the material for the whole.

Truly interesting this was. Most of the timbers required a slight curve in them, the exact curves being preserved in patterns, some of them dating from my grandfather's time, no doubt. Thus there was a pattern for the bottom-timbers of a waggon, and another for a dung-cart, and yet another for a "raved" cart. Waggon-shafts "off" and "near," cart-shafts, "hounds," "hames," tailboard rails, and a dozen other things, having to be cut to pattern, were first marked-out or "lined-out" on their respective planks, before the sawing could begin.

Tricky work it was, very often. Especially tricky, until you knew how, was lining-out the shafts for a cart. The pattern was not enough here. It gave the curve; but the outside width of the shafts at the back end where they fitted the cart, and the inside width the horse needed between them in front, introduced complications which had to be allowed for, before one shaft could be sawed out. So the lines had to be completed with chalk line and two-foot rule. I learnt how to do this years before I saw the reason for what was done. "Rule-of-thumb" was my guide, and as I suspect that this was all that the men had to go by, it may be supposed that it was a sort of folk tradition we were following each time we lined-out a pair of shafts.

There was a choice of two saws, but after a long time they both grew so dull that the men began to give broad hints of the need of the file. But not one of the staff offered to do the sharpening, probably because it was a mystery to them all. Indeed, sharpening the pit-saws had been my father's care. Accordingly, eager to fill his place wherever I could, I took on this job. To be sure, I had a little dim theory of what was wanted; I had watched the professional sawyer too; conceivably I was as likely to succeed at it as any of the wheelwrights. And at least I got a little "cut" into the saw. "She" felt right, when I passed my hand gently along the teeth, as I had seen the real sawyer do; yes, one felt a sort of bite from the newly filed teeth. And she looked right too, when I squinted along to see if the teeth stood out evenly in their two rows, this side and that. It is true, in the act of sawing afterwards an occasional jump of the saw almost jarred one's arms out and probably the top-sawyer swore a little, yet I do not recall any complaints. Only a facetious wheelwright took to calling one of the saws "Old Raspberry," in allusion to her scratching character. He also hinted that the teeth were "all uncles and aunts," they were so uneven.

If the one o'clock bell sounded before we had done, this same man was wont to say wearily: "Well, let's go and have some dinner. Perhaps we shall be stronger then." I wonder now—was that "just a thing to say"? or was he gibing at my physical weakness?. . .


## Learning the Trade

With the idea that I was going to learn everything from the beginning I put myself eagerly to boys' jobs, not at all dreaming that, at over twenty, the nerves and muscles are no longer able to put on the cell-growths, and so acquire the habits of perceiving and doing, which should have begun at fifteen. Could not Intellect achieve it? In fact, Intellect made but a fumbling imitation of real knowledge, yet hardly deigned to recognise how clumsy in fact it was. Beginning so late in life I know now I could never have earned my keep as a skilled workman. But, with the ambition to begin at the beginning, I set myself, as I have said, to act as boy to any of the men who might want a boy's help.

I recall one or two occasions when the men smiled to one another, not thinking I should see them smile; yet on the whole most kind they were, most helpful, putting me up to all sorts of useful dodges. The shriek of my saw against a hidden nail would bring the shop to a horrified standstill. When the saw jumped away from the cut I was trying to start, and jagged into my hand instead of into the timber, the men showed me where my hand ought to have been. Again, they taught me where to put my fingers, and how to steady my wrist against my knee, for chopping out wedges or "pins." Without this help, and if also my axe had been sharp enough (but that is unlikely), it would have been easy to chop off my fingers; with it I made better wedges than skilled men know how to make now, because with their machinery modern men are able to use material which anybody with an axe would know at a glance to be unfit. The men showed me how to drive in a nail without splitting the board yet without boring a hole for it to start. Wire nails had not then been introduced. "Rose-nails"—wrought iron, of slightly wedged shape—were the thing. By forcing it in the right direction a two-inch "cut-nail," as we called this kind, might be driven down to the very head, through inch elm into oak, with proper hammering. If sometimes a nail curled over instead of entering, or if it insisted on turning round so that the board was split after all, the fault was that the hammering was feeble or indirect. The men could not help that. They could not put into my wrist the knack that ought to have begun growing there five years earlier.

This same difficulty in hammering, which I never quite overcame, made me a poor hand at "knocking out dowels"—another job for boys. A dowel, with us, was a peg holding together the joints of a wheel-rim where the felloes meet. Heart of oak was not too tough for it; in fact, my father, superintending some spoke-cleaving, had carefully saved the very innermost cleft, all torn and ragged, for dowels. About the size and shape of a sausage, they were made by driving prepared lengths of oak through a "dowel cutter"—a sharp-edged ring of steel set in a block for that purpose, and a man with a heavy mallet could soon knock out a set of dowels. But, in my hand, the mallet was apt to fall a little sideways, so that the dowel, when finally slipping through on to the ground, proved crooked and useless.

Of course I had far too many irons in the fire—that was one part of the trouble. I was trying to learn four or five trades at once; and "intellect" fooled me by making them look simple. Indeed, so much of hand-work as intellect can understand does have that appearance, almost always to the undoing of the book-learned, who grow conceited. How simple is coal-hewing, fiddling, fishing, digging, to the student of books! I thought my business looked easy. Besides playing "boy" to the woodmen I went sometimes to help the blacksmith "shut" a tyre, and I always lent a hand at putting on tyres. Painters there were none, but as paint was used by the wheelwrights after they had finished a job, of course I came in for a little rough painting. I hadn't strength enough in my arm to grind up Prussian-blue for finishing a waggon-body. (Ah, the old muller and stone under the skylight in the loft, where in summer time one or two cabbage-butterflies would be fluttering! All the edges of the stone were thick-encrusted with dry paint, left behind by the flexible palette-knife and the shavings with which the middle of the stone was cleaned. The bench and the roof-beams all round were covered too with thick paint, where brushes had been "rubbed-out," for cleaning them, during many years.) I knew how to make putty, "knocking it up" with whiting and oil. I was familiar with "thinnings" of "turps," as we called turpentine. I kept watch on the kegs of dryers, Venetian-red, and so on, to see that paint was not drying on their sides but was kept properly scraped down into the covering puddle of water in the keg.

A number of duties fell on my shoulders in which nobody could guide me in my father's absence. During his illness and after his death I had to be master, as well as boy. Amongst other things was the work of store-keeper. Not only timber, iron and paint were wanted; axles and half-axles known as "arms" were kept in a corner of the body shop; and in my office, under lock and key, were the lighter kinds of hardware. Many times a day I was called away from my own job, whatever it might be, to get nails, screws, bolts, nuts, "ridgetie" chains, bolt-ends, "nut-heads," or what not. Sometimes, with hammer and "hard-chisel," I cut off lengths of chain for a tailboard, sometimes a longer length of a stouter chain for a "drag-bat," or of a slighter chain for a "roller." It was so small a shop that these interruptions were after all not too frequent. And anyhow I was proud to feel that I was doing what my father would have done. But of course I had to buy all the stores; to write orders for them or to interview commercial travellers; to overhaul invoices and pay the bills. As I said before, I do not remember that any commercial traveller ever tried to take advantage of my ignorance; but it is dreadful to think how much temptation I must have presented to them, running from saw-pit or smithy or paint-loft and aping the man of the world, in the hope that they might not notice anything odd about me.

Whenever a job was finished I went with slate to the men who had taken a hand in it, and wrote down what they had done to it, what materials they had used, and so on. Until I began to know the technical words, and the Surrey dialect of the men too, this was a great puzzle to me. How was I to know that when the old blacksmith spoke of a "roppin cleat" he had meant wrapping plate? or that a "shetlick" was the same thing that my father and grandfather spelt shutlock in the old ledger? The worst of it was that this gibberish (as it seemed to me) had to be charged up to customers. An uncle, long since dead, advised me to "charge enough and apologise"; but I have long known that I did not "charge enough." Hunting through the old ledger —my grandfather had started it—I was able to pick out and tabulate many customary prices. Not for many years did I introduce a proper system of "costing." In those old days there was a recognised price for much of the work. I believe that the figures were already antiquated and should have been bigger even at that far-away time; yet on the whole they served to keep things together while I was finding my feet. Customers seemed satisfied and continued sending work. Surely that meant that my charges were fair? It probably meant that they were found to be agreeably light. At any rate, the time came when I found out that most of the customers knew nothing about the meaning of the technical language of their wheelwright bills. Rather, they guessed what they would be called upon to pay and were pleased if I asked them for less—for they were surprisingly good judges of the price of things. Sometimes they complained—it was a principle with many—and enjoyed, I feel sure, the annoyance caused me. For I took it seriously, never dreaming that they were "pulling my leg." For my part I used to sigh, "How pleasant business might be were it not for customers!" . . .

## Prices

. . . Having no other guidance, I priced the work to my customers by my father's and my grandfather's charges, making schedules of figures from an old ledger. This plan was only not quite disastrous because, . . . there was in fact a local traditional price for new work and new parts, which nobody dared to exceed. This much was painfully proved to me long afterwards. A certain standard cart, I ascertained, was being sold throughout the neighbourhood at less than cost price. Accordingly I tried to get sundry rivals to join me in raising the price. One of these however made the project known to a good customer of mine and succeeded in getting that customer's work away from me. This was one of the many occasions when I should have welcomed pressure from a strong Trade Union, to compel other employers to make the changes I could not introduce alone.

My father had probably known for years how unprofitable some of the trade was. New work, he used to say, did not pay. Even in his time, and under his able management, it was only worth doing at all for the sake of keeping the staff together and getting the "jobbing"—the repairs; for, as there could be no standard in them, it was still possible to make a profit at jobbing.

On the subject of profits other tradesmen in the district were as ignorant and simple as myself. Although Farnham fancied itself a little town, its business was being conducted in the spirit of the village—almost indeed of the mediaeval manor. Men worked to oblige one another. Aldershot was almost as bad; Alton was if possible worse; and the most conservative village in the whole neighbourhood set the rate to which my own trade lived down. I doubt if there was a tradesman in the district— I am sure there was no wheelwright—who really knew what his output cost, or what his profits were, or if he was making money or losing it on any particular job. In later years, after the habit of giving estimates had become common (as it was unknown in 1884), I several times lost work to rivals who, I found out, were working for less than the mere iron and timber were to cost them. They never knew. Nor did they know if on to-morrow's estimate they were to make a fabulous profit. Well on into the present century these matters, in my trade, were settled by guess-work, not by calculation. We knew nothing, thought nothing, of how much we ought to have. But it was very needful to know how much our customer would pay.

This strange way of conducting business had possibly worked out well enough, say in Queen Anne's time when the shop was founded. In the course of generations errors would get corrected and a reasonable charge standardised. Neighbours, with little or no competition, would find out the fair prices of things and not dream of departing from them. Even in my grandfather's day the traditional prices would often hold good. Then, there were no "overhead" expenses—rates, fire-insurance, railway carriage, office charges, and so on—to compare with those of the present century. The wages left the employer a good margin. Thus, my grandfather paid but 17 s. a week where my father paid 24 s. Materials cost less.

But by the time I dropped into the business many changes had begun. Some of the old work was growing obsolete, unexampled work was coming into vogue all round. Not only was it

that "The Iron Age" . . . was on the move again, after years of
quiescence. Better roads, and imported foodstuffs too, broke up
the old farm-life on which my shop had waited. Instead of wag-
gons, vans to run twice as fast were wanted, and their springs
and brakes and lighter wheels revolutionised the industry my
men had taught me. At the same time the break-down of village
industries was introducing changes which were reflected in my
shop in the shape of butchers' carts and bread-carts—unknown
of old—and in brewers' drays and in millers' vans, not to mention vehicles for bricks and other building materials.

While novelties were pouring in upon the trade from one
side, on the other side an unexampled competition began to be
felt, keeping the prices still low. Things were not as in the
pre-railway days. Now, discontented customers would buy
"steam wheels" from London. Lighter wheels than any that
could be made in my shop—wheels imported ready-made from
America—had to be kept in stock along with the ancient sort of
naves and felloes. But the prices were effectually kept down
also by competition of another sort, or rather of a very ancient
sort. Dorset villages, Wiltshire villages, entered into the rivalry.
Thanks to their lower wages and rents, and their far less costly
timber, places one had never heard of were able to supply local
farmers at so cheap a rate that it was worth the farmers' while
to ignore, or to sacrifice, the advantage of vehicles made locally
with a view to local conditions. The circle of my competitiors
widened out by hundreds of miles.

In all these circumstances it is not wonderful that the price
of wheelwright's work by no means kept pace with the cost of
it. To tell the truth, the figures in my shop in 1884 (as extracted
by myself from the old books) were not much in excess of those
which Arthur Young found current in the southern counties in
1767. For a waggon the price had risen from about £21 then,
to £29 or £30 in my father's time; but carts, which at the later
date were but £12 or less, had averaged as much as £10 even
a century earlier.

Conceivably a man in so small a way of business as to do much of his work himself—and this must have been the case with many a village wheelwright—could make both ends meet even at these prices, even in 1884; and this the more if he got "jobbing" work to keep him going and to confuse his calculations. I knew one man who threw up a situation he had held for years in a rival's shop—probably under the impression that it was a profitable thing to be an employer even without capital; and began building new carts for a pound or so less than the local price. I am fairly certain that he kept no accounts to show him how much less his profits amounted to now than his weekly wages had been of old. Perhaps he never would have known this had there been plenty of repairs for him to do; but as it was, he had to close-down within twelve months, being too honest a man to profit by bankruptcy.

In these circumstances it is not surprising that I began at last to feel a need of some change or other. It is true, I knew nothing about "Costing." Methods for that were not devised until years later; but, in the simpler things, I did after four or five years— say in 1889—know well enough that some of the work was not paying its way—was even being done at a loss. Yet too often I saw work going elsewhere which I felt ought to have come to me. And one thing, if not certain, was probable: under my ignorant management the men had grown not so much lazy as leisurely. I knew this but too well; but I did not know how to mend the matter. Too early, indeed, I had realised how impossible it would be to carry out any of the Ruskinian notions, any of the fantastic dreams of profit-sharing, with which I had started. The men in the shop, eaten up with petty jealousies, would not have made any ideals work at all. But to discharge them was not to be thought of. How could I even find fault with those who had taught me what little I knew of the trade and who could but be only too well aware how little that was? Moreover, they were my friends. Business was troublesome enough even on the best of terms, but I could not have found the heart to go on with it all at the cost of the friction which must have come if I had begun trying to "speed-up" my friends and instructors. Meanwhile, none the less, the trade these friends of mine depended on for a living was slipping away, partly by their own fault.

What was to be done? How long I thought it over is more than I can at all tell now; but eventually—probably in 1889—I set up machinery: a gas-engine, with saws, lathe, drill and grindstone. And this device, if it saved the situation, was (as was long afterwards plain) the beginning of the end of the old style of business, though it did just bridge over the transition to the motor-trade of the present time.

I suppose it did save the situation. At any rate there was no need for dismissals, and after a year or two there was trade enough—of the more modern kind—to justify my engaging a foreman, whom I ultimately took into partnership. It proved a wise move from every point of view save the point of sentiment. The new head had experience and enterprise enough, without offending the men too, to develop the new commercial side— the manufacture of trade-vans and carts—when the old agricultural side of the business was dying out. Wood-work and iron-work were still on equal terms. Neither my partner nor myself realised at all that a new world (newer than ever America was to the Pilgrim Fathers) had begun even then to form all around us; we neither of us dreamt that the very iron age itself was passing away or that a time was actually near at hand when (as now) it would not be worth any young man's while to learn the ancient craft of the wheelwright or the mysteries of timber-drying. It might be that improved roads and plentiful building were changing the type of vehicles wheelwrights would have to build; but while horses remained horses and hill and valley were hill and valley, would not the old English provincial lore retain its value? We had no provocation to think otherwise, and yet:—

And yet, there in my old-fashioned shop the new machinery

had almost forced its way in—the thin end of the wedge of scientific engineering. And from the first day the machines began running, the use of axes and adzes disappeared from the well-known place, the saws and saw-pit became obsolete. We forgot what chips were like. There, in that one little spot, the ancient provincial life of England was put into a back seat. It made a difference to me personally, little as I dreamt of such a thing. "The Men," though still my friends, as I fancied, became machine "hands." Unintentionally, I had made them servants waiting upon gas combustion. No longer was the power of horses the only force they had to consider. Rather, they were under the power of molecular forces. But to this day the few survivors of them do not know it. They think "Unrest" most wicked.

Yet it must be owned that the older conditions of "rest" have in fact all but dropped out of modern industry. Of course wages are higher—many a workman to-day receives a larger income than I was ever able to get as "profit" when I was an employer. But no higher wage, no income, will buy for men that satisfaction which of old—until machinery made drudges of them—streamed into their muscles all day long from close contact with iron, timber, clay, wind and wave, horse-strength. It tingled up in the niceties of touch, sight, scent. The very ears unawares received it, as when the plane went singing over the wood, or the exact chisel went tapping in (under the mallet) to the hard ash with gentle sound. But these intimacies are over. Although they have so much more leisure men can now taste little solace in life, of the sort that skilled hand-work used to yield to them. Just as the seaman to-day has to face the stoke-hole rather than the gale, and knows more of heat-waves than of sea-waves, so throughout. In what was once the wheelwright's shop, where Englishmen grew friendly with the grain of timber and with sharp tool, nowadays untrained youths wait upon machines, hardly knowing oak from ash or caring for the qualities of either. And this is but one tiny item in the immensity of changes which have overtaken labour throughout the civilised world.

The products of work are, to be sure, as important as ever—what is to become of us all if the dockers will not swear for us or the miners risk their lives? That civilisation may flourish a less-civilised working-class must work. Yet others wonder at working-class "unrest." But it remains true that in modern conditions work is nothing like so tolerable as it was say thirty years ago; partly because there is more hurry in it, but largely because machinery has separated employers from employed and has robbed the latter of the sustaining delights which materials used to afford to them. Work is less and less pleasant to do—unless, perhaps, for the engineer or the electrician.

But, leaving these large matters, I would speak of a smaller one. Is there—it is worth asking—such laughter about labour, such fun, such gamesome good temper, as cheered the long hours in my shop in 1884? Are we not taking industry too seriously to be sensible about it? Reading of "Scientific Management" I recall something quite different from that—something friendly, jolly, by no means scientific—which reached down to my time from an older England. A mischievous spirit itself freshened one up sometimes. One day there came, knocking at my office-door, an innocent apprentice-boy with a message from the wheelwright who was teaching him his trade. "Please sir," the boy said, "Mr —— sent me to get a straight hook." Of course I ought to have been angry with the man for wasting time in sending the boy off on a fool's errand, and with the boy for coming to me when he must assuredly have been sent to the blacksmiths. But in fact I could not be angry. I sent the boy back. "Go and tell Mr —— if he wants a straight hook to come and ask me for it himself."

And though there cannot have been any profit in that transaction I have always valued the good temper it betokened all round, as a product of industry too much overlooked in modern times. There ought really to be a little fun in work, for the workman's sake. And I think he will insist on it, even at the cost of a little less Civilisation for the Employing Classes.

# 4

# THE END OF THE ROAD FOR THE SKILLED WORKER: Automaking at Renault

## Alain Touraine

Touraine's book on changes in work at Renault began as an M.A. thesis for the Sorbonne, written in 1949. A revised version was published in 1955. The book soon became a classic, and Touraine has been acknowledged as the most brilliant sociologist now writing in France. Currently the director of the Center for the Study of Social Movements at the Ecole Pratique des Hautes Etudes, the author has passed from history and sociology of industry as such to the study of conflicts between entire classes and cultures in modern society.

Renault's central works, located on an island in the Seine within the Parisian suburb of Billancourt, is the largest single factory in France today. It was also the country's first great enterprise to adopt assembly-line production.

I included this reading in order to illustrate two themes: (1) the persistence of skilled artisanal labor within the factory system until a relatively late date; (2) the precise ways in which assembly-line work differs from craftwork. But the reader should note that the principal skill in question, that of the ma-

SOURCE: Alain Touraine, *L'Evolution du travail ouvrier aux usines Renault* (Paris: Centre National de la Recherche Scientifique, 1955), pp. 57–74. Reprinted with permission of the author. My translation.

chinist, virtually did not exist in traditional society and was created by mechanized factory industry.

## The Rise of the Machinist

Even if nowadays the automobile industry, by virtue of assembly-line work, has largely done away with skilled mechanics, we mustn't forget that at the same time the industry gave these men an importance they had never previously known.

It's hard to make out the exact course of events in the nineteenth and twentieth centuries. Before the rise of the mechanical construction industry, of which automaking is just one part, metalworking shops with machinery were very few in number. In drawing his picture of industry under the Second Empire, Georges Duveau, for example, leaps in a single bound from blast furnaces, forges, and foundries to small ironmongery and hardware. This is too rapid a transition, for the railways, the shipbuilding industry, and the manufacture of machines and looms employed in various other industrial sectors all presupposed the existence of machine shops and of skilled production machinists. But such shops were few, and alongside the machinists and lathe operators were to be found, in much greater number, fitters and skilled handworkers, forge operators, blacksmiths, metalsmiths, carpenters, and so on. The machinist was even considered inferior to the fitter; he was essentially charged with roughing down, for it was the task of the fitter to finish up, in his vise, metal parts which had just been sketched out by machine.

Most mechanics who worked with machines were not employed on production lines but in the adjacent tool shops, as for example in textile mills. Louis-René Villermé [an investigator of social conditions during the July Monarchy], in visiting a cotton-printing mill, distinguished among three skill categories: the engravers, who fashioned the wooden plates used in hand printing; the printers, whose skill level, though always rudimentary, depended on whether they worked by hand or at a machine; and the laborers. Other machinists, such as wood and metal lathe operators, were needed in the textile industry for building and repairing equipment. Such jobs represented in these mills, three-quarters inhabited by women and children, a refuge for skilled work, but their proportion was small. The mass production textile industry was already in the phase of assembly-line manufacture, the effects of which were accentuated and aggravated by capitalist competition—this at a time when the mechanical construction industry scarcely existed.

The appearance of the automobile industry is one of the first signs of the birth of the skilled production worker: automobiles give a fundamental importance to the mechanic working on machines; automobiles organize the shop for the first time not around the fitter, not around the skilled artisan working by hand with the aid of his tools, but around the machinist.

The skilled machinist constituted at Renault the backbone of the work force until the period of war production (1914–1918), or indeed until 1924, when the assembly line was introduced at Billancourt. And it is today not the artisan or the toolmaker whom the old foremen have in mind when they deplore the decline of skill levels among the journeymen, but the machinist.

Yet keep in mind that around 1910 the development of machining represented for the mechanics a decline in occupational status. The machinist is, in essence, constrained to repetitive, even monotonous work; he therefore specializes, and his knowledge and competence drop below those of a fitter or a toolmaker. Even when the machinist, paid at piece rates, makes ten or twenty centimes an hour more than the toolmaker, who is paid by the hour, he envies him, for even the incentive of a higher wage would not push the toolmaker to do production work at a lathe or a milling machine. Toolmaking is more varied; it permits a man to develop his talents; it constantly challenges the mind. "On the contrary, the skilled production worker ends up being ground down. Thus the stimulation of the work and the occupational *amour-propre* of toolmaking ensure that even the machinist himself places such jobs above the class of machine operators" [E. Riché, *La situation des ouvriers dans l'industrie automobile*, Paris, 1909].

But in narrow terms of worker competence as such, the automobile has *raised* the skill level of the machinist. Even if the contemporary machinist remains inferior to the toolmaker, he is superior to the machinist of an earlier epoch, for the machines that he uses are more elaborate and the tolerances they permit narrower. This development is even more marked in foundries. "Foundry production in former days consisted of objects with very simple molds, such as pans or pot-bellied stoves. The automobile changed fundamentally this state of things. It asked the foundries to start making motor parts on the basis of highly complex molds, the execution of which demanded extreme skill and care. The more so as the molds changed ceaselessly with each new improvement that the automakers built into their vehicles." [Ibid.]

Thus the beginning of the automobile industry marked in practice the beginning of a new type of occupation—machinist. In the middle of the nineteenth century mechanical construction was still being done by artisanal methods where the subdivision of labor was elementary; machines played only a secondary role. But with the automobile, a new kind of industrial sector and a new kind of skilled worker appeared. The birth of a new industry (which would pass progressively from custom work to mass production) had conjoined with the appearance of a new type of worker.


## The Machinist's Skill

The machinist's usefulness to an employer lies in his skill. Machines make possibilities available to the machinist: it's up to him to take advantage of them. Because many machines have slow rates of depreciation, the workshops are full of ancient milling machines and lathes, imprecise and poorly adjusted. The worker must know what his machine is capable of, how to wheedle and coax precision out of it. The worker "makes do." He may shore up the frame here or there to take out the play, reestablishing the horizontal alignment for better results in milling. The company cannot retool completely for each new product line. The production machinist must himself take the initiative in readying the old machines. He has his personal little tool kit, consisting of calipers and wedges. He must know something of handwork, of how to use a file, for many of the parts he is to turn out are so complicated that they can only be roughed down by machine. Hand finishing is required.

Lacking a theoretical understanding of metallurgy and of metalwork, the machinist is guided solely by his personal experience. The wood molder himself chooses the stock; the wood turner can feel the vibration in a poorly executed piece, into which the bit has cut too deeply. To finish a job he might take a drawing knife in his hands, resting the handle against his shoulder and the other end of the knife against the workbench so that the cutting edge is just slightly beneath the shaft of the piece he is finishing. He then goes to work with this entire body; he feels in his bones just how the tool is performing.

The old drill presses were called "Nervous Nellies." The operator, just as the turner, had constantly to adjust his machine, adapting it with careful little movements to the nature of the metal and of the assignment. And even after the appearance of the tool carriage, the machinist had constantly to be alert, every sense sharpened.

It is immediately obvious how the machinist is different from the semiskilled worker of today. But at the same time, the machinist is quite different from the artisan or the mechanic of the nineteenth century. He is not independent; his work rhythms are not free. His manual skills are nullified by the machine's inadequacies and are no longer the basis of his qualification. He still estimates, but he has to measure as well. The wood turners at Renault are constrained to a preciseness of which the artisanal turners in the Faubourg Saint-Antoine [a quarter of Paris which had many small workshops] knew nothing. Even though mass production may not yet have arrived, the tolerances are very narrow, given the machines available. A motor consists of a large number of parts; how would they fit together if each did not conform to an exact model? Hence the measuring and the calculating. The artisan, who has before him all the parts of the object he is manufacturing, can rely on the rule of thumb, assembling the pieces by trial and error, fiddling with those which don't fit. But the machinist has to hand over a part that will fit with all the other parts, which have been fashioned in other shops and which he never sees. The coordination of production presupposes rigor. It is the machine and precise measurement, not the personal judgment and "the eye," which in the end supply interchangeable parts. The skill of the worker no longer consists in attaining the desired result through his own techniques, but in placing himself at the service of a machine, submitting himself to its rhythms and its limitations. The machine is in command.

Outside of the machine shop events take different forms but the same direction. The changes in forging are similar to those in machining. They lead from the blacksmith working by hand to the stamping-machine operator. The power of the human body, the precision of movement and eye, are the essence of the stereotype Emile Zola gives us in *l'Assomoir*. The good worker doing a good job. Even with a steam hammer it is still the skill of the smith that determines the quality of the work. But things are different with the stamping machine. To be sure, the work is still arduous, but the worker's skill consists solely in placing the metal blank in the indentation which the machine will strike. The worker serves the machine. There is nothing automatic in his task; constant attentiveness is required, but he loses the sense of working directly with the materials of nature.

In the foundries, hand molding demands considerable

manual skill. Care, precision, and dexterity are the essence of the molder's work. And throughout early industrialization this job scarcely changed. The tools remain elementary, manipulated by hand (even if a pneumatic press is available). But the machines of advanced industrialization deal a brutal death blow to hand molding. . . .

Enough manual work remains to make these occupations arduous still. The molder must work bent over the mold or perhaps flat on his back. The polisher must often hold a heavy piece before the machine, forced to manipulate it rapidly in the dust-filled room. Even the machinist must carry about heavy parts in the absence of mechanical conveyors. Similar in this regard to the artisan, early factory workers throw all of themselves into their work.

## Training and Tradition

The importance of manual skill, especially in crafts where mechanization has not yet penetrated, presupposes a slow process of training, through watching, through doing, and through tradition.

The foundry worker in department 63, who decides by looking at the color of the flame (often ignoring the pyrometer) whether the metal is ready for pouring—important in terms of avoiding costly overheats—took a long time to learn about metals. Metal casting at the Saint-Michel-de-Maurienne plant is a six-hour operation, different each time because of constant variation in assignments. The chief founder, who must successively charge the furnace with scrap iron, smelt the iron, refine and dephosphorize the charge (being careful to avoid the formation of carbon), add carbon, manganese, and nickel, then— after having removed the slag a second time—add cobalt or some other rare metal, and finally bring the metal up to a given temperature and pour it, can assume such responsibilities only after having worked for many years on the furnace as a second assistant, a first assistant, and then a stoker.

In the steel rolling mills, the chief cutter, whose job it is to turn the ingot and shove it onto the train of rollers, will have worked first on the slabs of metal as a common hand, helping to cut the bars as they shoot off the train, before progressing from assistant trimmer, to transporter, to stoker, and finally to chief cutter.

Before the Astier Law (July 1919), the apprentice machinist was trained in the workshop itself, under the supervision of a master who was frequently his father. He helped out the master, relieving him of secondary tasks, doing odd jobs for him, and learning from him the principles of the craft, which is to say acquiring the manual skills that would permit him to perform a whole range of affiliated crafts. There are no metal turners who don't also know how to countersink and bore; there are no molders who aren't capable of shaping the largest as well as the smallest pieces and of casting them as well. The importance of skill thus entails the polyvalence of the workers.

The skilled worker on whose shoulders production rests is not therefore isolated in the shop. His control stretches over an assistant, an apprentice, or several laborers. And especially in mechanical construction, a group of skilled workers will be aided by a gang of "kids" and some unskilled laborers. In both cases the skilled worker is at the core of a primary group.

This phenomenon is not peculiar to mechanical construction; it is to be found everywhere in early industrialization. Work is done in small teams, constituted about a chief production worker who is not in the slightest comparable to the foreman of assembly-line work, a representative of management. This central figure is sometimes called "the chief" [*l'ouvrier*]. In the old glassworks the chief is assisted by a first blower, a second blower, a headboy, and a second boy, without counting the stoker and the charger—men independent of the chief. That is also the organization in traditional coal mines, where the hewer who runs the team is called "chief," and is assisted by an aide, a younger digger, and a hauler, without counting the timbermen, repairers, stowers, and stonemen, who come in occasionally to work under his supervision.

The chief's authority stems not merely from his place in a hierarchy; it rests upon his age, his experience, and his occupational skill. This division between formal and informal organization, so characteristic of mass-production work, is known neither in the plants of early industrialization nor in the small shops of traditional society. And the solidarity of these small groups, so beloved of American sociology, is guaranteed (relatively) by the fact that the chief has chosen the men he wants to work with him.

Such teamwork would appear to reserve the most important and the most demanding tasks for the skilled workers. But, in fact, the diversity of the job and the absence of a permanent, rationalized organizational chart mean that skilled and unskilled tasks are inextricably intermixed. Beyond his regular duties, and in addition to the time he needs to improve his techniques and to seek out better materials and tools, the skilled worker devotes a good part of his day to ancillary tasks, unskilled but necessary to set the job up.

In the coal mines around the turn of the century, the head hewer would spend the first half of his day in coal getting, either by pick or by blasting. After lunch (and especially when dynamite had been used), he would switch tasks, knocking apart large lumps, sorting out the rocks which had slipped in amongst the coal, loading the carts, putting in the timbers—assisted in all these tasks by his helpers. And even if the subdivision of labor were more advanced, the head hewer would still have to drill in the dynamite and make sure the coal was removed from the face, during the time he was not occupied with coal-getting itself.

Different again is the example of the steam locomotive engineer. He must similarly spend a good deal of his time in unskilled tasks, preliminary or auxiliary to his regular work. Checking the locomotive out and, indeed, the ritual progression from routing office to lantern room takes at least an hour of time and involves perhaps eighty separate operations for an average locomotive. At the end of a run, he still has to fill up the tender with coal and sand, and, before leaving the roundhouse, bring the locomotive up to the pit for servicing.

The diversity of the job, his freedom to operate as he pleases, the absence of any kind of standardization all leave to the worker enormous initiative. There is in early industrialization little lathe work that can be done in exactly the same manner for a series of parts. And for the locomotive engineer, no run is exactly the same as the previous. Professional competency consists in the possession of a thousand different little things one has to know, trade secrets which don't leave the shop and which are transmitted from generation to generation, which the craftsman alone is to know and which he passes on to but a sole individual.

The former metallurgist was like an alchemist, hiding what he did in the mixing vats from his helpers, a precaution which failed to prevent a good deal of early industrial espionage.

Rational shop organization has caused much of this arcane, traditional lore to disappear. Trade secrets, however, are still preserved here and there. Such and such a department head fails to pass on some procedure that was imparted to him long ago, lore which perhaps will soon be no longer necessary, but which guarantees him his position for the time being. The importance of these traditions is such that the director of Renault's foundries can say, even today, that good molders are no longer being trained in the Paris region, that it's necessary to go and hunt them out in the "iron country," the Ardennes, the Haute-Marne, or at Le Creusot. In the Saint-Michel plant the best workers come from Champagnole, where aging steelworkers have trained the local labor force and passed onto it the traditional lore of steelmaking.

## Initiative and Technical Knowledge

The absence of formal training programs, the role of practiced dexterity and of trade secrets transmitted by experience, the importance of knowing intimately the raw materials and of developing the faculties by doing—all affirm the empirical, non-technical nature of the machinist's skills. They get along by guess and by gosh. The wood turners of Renault's department 26 devise for themselves a whole series of little mounting blocks for the rapid centering of their pieces. Similarly, the milling-machine operators of department 27 hang onto the special tools they fix up for the most frequent kinds of jobs, which means that, in fact, they end up specializing in whatever job they happen to have tools for. This explains the specialization of the machinists and the diversity to be found within their ranks. Even though they may be multicompetent within their craft, these machinists cannot alternate jobs, whereas an unskilled production worker, who is familiar only with a certain kind of machine, can be more easily transferred to another productive sector where what little he knows about geometry and machine work permit him rapidly to adapt himself. A high number of skilled specialists is more characteristic of early industrialization, where wage differentials exist not merely between skilled and unskilled, but among the skilled themselves, and differences of even a few centimes in hourly rates betoken differences in skill among the workers (and in the demand *for* workers as well).

Intuitive work is still possible in some settings, impossible in others. It is still a rule at the forge. Even though the old hands know how to read a set of specifications, they rarely use them, preferring to work from a sketch and letting the foreman show them the required metal weights and permitted tolerances. Intuition is still dominant at the rolling mill, where the workers operate more often from a clay model than from written specifications. But such rule-of-thumb work suits poorly the men who must operate lathes and milling machines. They must work from specifications; they must understand the principles by which their machines operate; they must in consequence possess a true "technical" competence [as opposed to an artisanal, handwork competence]. This competence will increase as the need for precision and the polyvalence of the machines themselves increase.

If this machinist does not historically represent an intermediate stage between the old craftsman and the machine operator of the huge modern factory, he nonetheless combines some of the qualities of each, more of a technician than was the craftsman, more of a skilled traditional handworker and less technological than the contemporary operative.

Such are, in broad outline, the features of the skilled machinist. It was first in the automobile industry that he appeared; it was the automobile industry which transformed the nature of work among the other crafts. His arrival signifies the direct intervention of machines in the productive process. Abandoning their subordinate role, machines come to take on assignments ever more precise, becoming themselves ever more complex, increasingly perfect, so that in productive work they end up having little in common with primitive machines. One thinks of the transformation of the primitive lathe or milling machine to the "complex universal machine." The multiplicity of the jobs such machines can do means the operator can choose among the various techniques he knows, guided by his personal experience and by the traditions of his craft.

This variety of mechanization effects a number of changes in the skill structure of the industry. In between the laborers and the toolmakers, but closer to the latter, the skilled production workers begin to mushroom, elbow to elbow with the laborers, assisted by them and by the apprentices, but performing tasks of exacting skill.

The fitter is the best representative of this era. He does handwork, owning a vast variety of files, scrappers, and planes, yet is familiar as well with machines; he is able to countersink, plane, mortice—even to work a milling machine or a lathe.

In the capacity of production machinist, he is free in the choice of methods he adopts; he designs, plans ahead, organizes his own work; machines occupy a well-defined, subordinate place in the overall setup. Even today, a senior fitter in department 5 will have to devise on his own the mounting for a job which involes boring two parts simultaneously. Research and development, overwhelmed by the task of getting out the 4 CV [Renault's enormously popular small car], did not have the time to design the required mounting. The fitter determines the tools to be used, the procedures to adopt, seeking out himself the necessary materials for the job. Other work in the shop— the simple processing of parts coming off an automatic lathe— represents a stunning contrast to his own: the gestures are rapid, the task monotonous. His sort of work involves considerable reflection, going off in search of metal bars and sheet steel, working successively at a number of machines, and then fitting for size the construction he has just put together. The role of the machine is not the same; the rhythm of work is different. A job once begun by such a worker cannot be completed by another. The work is personalized.

## The Decline and Fall of the Skilled Crafts: Technological Factors

What remains of the shop hand of yesteryear, of this skilled worker who, even in the auto assembly rooms, handled the greatest part of the machine work?

A number of skilled workers are still to be found at Renault. Let us ignore for a moment the tool shops. In 1948, 19 percent of the workers in the machine shops were skilled; 29 percent in equipment, 27 percent in the other departments involving handwork. And only a small proportion of these men were machine-setters. Even in many departments devoted to assembly some skilled hands remained.

But after 1914–1918, the progressive elimination of skilled workers began in most of the assembly shops, a consequence of the defense contracts of the War. This entailed the complete overturn of the structure of work at Renault.

But at the same time that the number of skilled hands dropped off, the number of unskilled laborers diminished too. Between the two groups stepped a new category, the "semi-skilled" workers [in French *ouvriers spécialisés*, or "O.S." for short]. Skilled labor took refuge in either the setting up of jobs, toolmaking, or maintenance and repair, all of which were located in segregated shops. These skilled equipment experts are very different from the skilled production workers who continue to exist here and there in the line shops. Thus complications appear: in place of the skilled machinist and the laborer, working side by side on a job, there appear varieties of workers who have only indirect, abstract contacts with one another.

This new kind of organization did not happen overnight, and even today remnants of the early industrial system of organization are visible alongside the modern order. The majority of shops in the Billancourt plant however typify mass-production manufacturing.

The proliferation and specialization of machinery entailed in mass-production have accelerated the subdivision of labor, the replacement of a single worker, whose job was varied (and performed with "flexible" machines), by a number of workers executing parcelled, repetitive tasks with specialized machines. The proportion of handwork diminishes: the file gives way to the drill press and the milling machine. Machine work itself becomes subdivided into simple steps, the execution of which requires but the briefest training, a matter of days devoted more to adapting the worker to the new rhythms of work than to actual instruction. The shapes of the parts become ever sim-

pler, in order to reduce the amount of handwork and to facilitate the tooling of jobs.

Mass production both requires and permits completely interchangeable parts. It was not the automobile which first stum-
bled upon this principle. Interchangeability originated in printing shops, and it was the proliferation of small machines,
especially of sewing machines, which made interchangeability
one of the hallmarks of modern industry. But the automobile
generalized and systematized the principle.

Interchangeability demands from all concerned rigorous discipline and submission to given directives. The initiative of the
individual worker is almost completely suppressed. The general
organization of work, the methods to be employed, sometimes
even the gestures to be performed, are all determined by systems managers, and in particular by the time-motion office. The
tooling up of a job, final guarantor of precision, is taken from the
worker and assigned to a special service.

This replacement of unified work by assembly-line work, of
individualized methods by closely clocked standardized operations, is not just limited to the assembly shops; it extends even
to the repair shops. In many cases defective parts are no longer
repaired, no longer patched back into service; it is more efficient simply to throw them onto the scrap heap and take a new
part off the line. More generally, "repairing" acquires a new
connotation: formerly it entailed restoring a worn out or broken
part; now it involves replacement by a new part.

The rationalization of the plant has decreased the time required to exchange the parts in a car. The replacement of a
connecting rod requires three hours for the 4 CV instead of the
six and one-half hours for the old Celtaquatre [a previous Renault model]. Taking out and replacing the generator now takes
fifteen minutes instead of an hour and a quarter. The complete
dismantling of the rear axle now requires an hour instead of
three and one-half hours, thus gains of 54 percent, 83 percent

and 71 percent. And there's more: the standard exchange system permits a garage to send back to the factory the entire defective unit, replacing it with another complete unit, ready for installation. The old unit will be renovated and, in turn, installed in another car. This system results not only in considerable time savings to the customer, but in a drastic transformation of repair personnel. Skilled workers become increasingly scarce in garages, and are concentrated instead in the large factories. At the same time, the former skilled factory workers are replaced by other less qualified hands, or by semiskilled operatives. . . .

Thus the objective of standardized, rationalized mass production is not necessarily mechanical perfection, in some abstract sense, but the elimination of skilled labor from the assembly line. The machines are simple, permitting a swift work pace and low production costs. Handwork means lost time, the interruption of the work flow, and high costs.

## The Decline and Fall of the Skilled Crafts: Social Factors

To these economic considerations must be added several interconnected social factors. French industry has experienced within certain sectors a shortage of skilled workers. In pursuit of self-interest, French industrialists have frequently failed to train apprentices or to give job instruction to their own workers, hoping to find on the open market an adequate number of skilled hands. Or else management has insured that the training was very narrow, thereby linking the workers to the companies and safeguarding against a loss of their investment. Even at Renault, the head of a department told me about his effort to specialize the solderers, who until that time (1949) had worked on all grades of metals. Thus specialized, these men would no longer be able to leave Renault for smaller shops which demanded utility solderers.

One author, the administrator of a large mechanical construction plant, wrote on the subject of training courses, "Many workers, without leaving the company and with the approval of management, ended up with a different qualification than they had envisaged at the program's beginning. Either because they discovered special aptitudes or because the company needed immediately certain categories of workers, these men profited from the chance to specialize."[1] He went on to say, "In apprenticeship one looks to the training of a polyvalent worker, and to this end courses and technical instruction play a large role. But in the regular training of adults, or of youth who do not have contracts, training is primarily in manual operations." Thus production calls the tune.

Moreover, skilled workers have always represented the most militant part of the working class, and employers have not been reluctant to eliminate as much as possible such malcontents from their plants. Another author cites a characteristic example from foundry work: molders doing automobile assignments were better paid than the others. Consequently getting workers for other jobs became ever more difficult, just as the automobile molders' wage demands became ever more annoying. The molding machine, introduced after 1906, first permitted the mechanical execution of simple jobs, then made possible automobile work too. Soon the hand molders were reduced to a choice between unemployment and the status of machine operatives. Thus in the interwar period, what is known as the "contortment of occupational skill" became general.

### The End of the Road: Exhaustion and Dispersal

All these technical and economic factors tend to eliminate skilled workers from production lines. On the whole this elimi-

[1]F. Neil, *La Formation professionelle dans les enterprises de la mécanique* . . . (Paris, 1948), p. 29.

nation has taken place as two separate processes: the decay and
the disappearance of the old crafts. But it would nonetheless not
be entirely accurate to sce this process just as the replacement
of the former skilled craftsmen by either craftsmen of a lesser
quality or by semiskilled laborers. Events have taken a subtler
course.

A certain number of crafts have already disappeared, or are
about to do so, some of them in consequence of the obsoles-
cence of the raw material they used. The progressive reduction
of wood in autobodies entailed a continuing decline in skilled
woodworking crafts at Renault. Other crafts disappeared as a
result of the abandonment of the procedures and methods they
utilize, such as handcraft trades doomed by mechanization. At
the present time, one such craft is in its death throes at Renault:
the tinsmiths. In the radiator shop of department 38, where
developments have been delayed by the Second World War
and by the allied bombardments, the production line is adequate, and many parts are still turned out by hand, by tinsmiths.
But their number has been slowly diminishing. Other tinsmiths
are at work in department 12 on gas tanks for trucks. But their
jobs, which in reality are those of tin solderers, are threatened
by the automatic welding machine. Shortly, truck gas tanks will
be made by a stamping machine, as happens now with 4 CV gas
tanks. As a premonition of the doom of this craft, the department's semiskilled workers who want to learn a trade choose to
become sheet-iron workers, not tinsmiths.

The forge worker, swinging his hammer against the anvil, is
also on the way out. There are scarcely a handful left in the
forge department. Only slightly more remain in the central
toolshop. On the production lines the disappearance of these
men is almost complete; Renault no longer trains apprentices
in forging.

The file worker has completely vanished, replaced by a machine. Other men had specialized in cleaning the banks of
lathes; the "superfinishing" process meant the end of them.
Skilled cementation workers have given way to semiskilled

hands. All these disappearances entail the devaluation of the work process. . . .

Thus some crafts die slowly, gradually asphyxiated by the advance of the machine and plant rationalization. Others, however, perish in sudden death. The example of hand molders in Renault's foundries is typical, for here no skilled worker using a machine intervened between the stages of handwork and of mass production.

The collapse of molding took place before the introduction of machines, through the simple act of the subdivision of labor. Even though the small-shop molder, assisted by several laborers, had been able to accomplish the most varied tasks, in big plants even before 1914 production had to be carved up among specialists. In a shipbuilding yard in 1903, for example, there were already five categories of workers in the iron foundry: molders and pattern makers, toolmakers, foundrymen and their assistants, fettlers, and laborers. This was still an elementary subdivision of labor, even though molding, pattern making, and the chipping of the mold are already distinct. (The presence of toolmakers in a production workshop is, on the contrary, an anachronism which dates from the shops of the nineteenth century.)

This subdivision of labor accelerated during the First World War. In 1919 the composition of the personnel in Renault's foundry was as follows:

| | |
|---|---|
| Foremen | 13 |
| Salaried employees | 7 |
| Machine operators | 14 |
| Pattern makers | 17 |
| Molders | 75 |
| Engravers | 29 |
| Welders | 9 |
| Checkers | 40 |
| Various | 31 |
| Furnacemen | 11 |

| | |
|---|---|
| Maintenance workers | 23 |
| Laborers | 78 |
| Women | 48 |

The high number of laborers indicates the survival of traditional work methods. The presence of machine operators is quite new, but numerically still unimportant. The principal phenomenon is the growing specialization in skilled tasks, and above all the proliferation of nonskilled workers (such as checkers, "various," and furnacemen) who are nonetheless distinct from laborers.

It is only with the appearance of assembly-line production, after 1924, that the subdivision of labor ended in the complete dissolution of the craft of molder and its replacement by specialized jobs: one man who readies the mold, another who clamps it, another who dumps it out, and so on. . . .

Today in major foundries, hand molders are used only in the fabrication of special orders. In such cases it is impossible for the company to do a time-motion study, impossible to supervise the pace of work, the number of breaks taken. The company must rely on the competence and integrity of the individual worker.

The skilled foundry worker has been similarly replaced by a number of workers, either semiskilled hands or skilled men whose competence is less complete than his own. The tasks that he took on, with the help of his assistants, are now rigorously subdivided among the man who prepares the charge for the furnace, bringing up the pig iron, the scrap metal, the coke, the flux, and so on, weighing the material and loading it into tip trucks; the man who dumps the charge into the mouth of the furnace and spreads it out with a fire rake; the foundryman as such, who has retained as functions merely the breaking of the bloc which obstructs the taphole, the resealing of the hole after the pour with the help of a slate cone, the supervision of the level of metal in the crucible, and the removal of the slag; one mason, who patches up damage to the furnace walls; another mason who scrapes off stubborn residues of slag, puts in new

blocs, and handles the baking-in; the pourer who, having filled
the ladles with molten metal, hustles them over to the molds
and fills them up; and the man who monitors the pyrometer. In
this fashion, specialization has taken the place of variety. Instead of lodging in the single person of the master foundryman,
as in days past, occupational skill has been broken up. The
rationalization of production has diminished worker initiative.
Work is done with precise directives and not according to traditions and to instinct. The crafts of the foundry have thus col-
lapsed.

# 5

# INSIDE THE NEW YORK TELEPHONE COMPANY

## Elinor Langer

This reading addresses at least two interesting problems, that of the white-collar proletariat and that of the destruction of meaning in work through bureaucratization. The women who work for "Ma Bell" in New York City are by any conventional definition a proletariat: they are all equally unskilled and in a common situation vis-à-vis their employer; their jobs are monotonous and repetitive; they are poorly paid; and from the fruits of their labor the New York Telephone Company is able to distribute handsome dividends. The characteristic of a classical proletariat which they lack, however, is collective consciousness of their plight. For in this and in a subsequent essay in the *New York Review of Books* Langer makes clear that these women do not consider themselves to be exploited, nor are they willing to act together to improve their condition. One recognizes here the familiar problem of the white-collar proletariat: objectively exploited, subjectively its members believe themselves more likely to improve their lot through individual than through collective action. Or for other reasons these new proletarians fail to mobilize themselves, and lapse into indifference.

SOURCE: Elinor Langer, "Inside the New York Telephone Company (I)," *New York Review of Books*, vol. 14, no. 5 (March 12, 1970). Reprinted with permission of the International Famous Agency.

Their "exploitation" and "proletarianism" are matters still open for discussion. What is indisputable, however, is the meaninglessness of the work. These are jobs from which all autonomy, all variety, all sense of participation and creativity have been drained. The assembly line's subdivision of labor and bureaucratization of authority find their mirror image in the white-collar world of New York Tel. And in stepping through this mirror we leave behind definitively the small-shop artisans of traditional society.

From October to December 1969 I worked for the New York Telephone Company as a Customer's Service Representative in the Commercial Department. My office was one of several in the Broadway City Hall area of lower Manhattan, a flattened, blue-windowed commercial building in which the telephone company occupies three floors. The room was big and brightly lit—like the city room of a large newspaper—with perhaps one hundred desks arranged in groups of five or six around the desk of a Supervisor. The job consists of taking orders for new equipment and services and pacifying customers who complain, on the eleven exchanges (although not the more complex business accounts) in the area between the Lower East Side and 23rd Street on the North and bounded by Sixth Avenue on the West.

My Supervisor is the supervisor of five women. She reports to a Manager who manages four supervisors (about twenty women) and he reports to the District Supervisor along with two other managers. The offices of the managers are on the outer edge of the main room separated from the floor by glass partitions. The District Supervisor is down the hall in an executive suite. A job identical in rank to that of the district Supervisor is held by four other men in Southern Manhattan alone. They report to the Chief of the Southern Division, himself a soldier in an army of division chiefs whose territories are the five boroughs, Long Island, Westchester, and the vast hinterlands vaguely referred to as "Upstate." The executives at —— — Street were only dozens among the thousands in New York Tel alone.

Authority in their hierarchy is parceled out in bits. A Representative, for example, may issue credit to customers up to, say, $10.00; her supervisor, $25.00; her manager, $100.00; his supervisor, $300.00; and so forth. These employees are in the same relation to the centers of power in AT&T and the communications industry as the White House guard to Richard Nixon. They all believe that "The business of the telephone company is Service" and if they have ever heard of the ABM or AT&T's relation to it, I believe they think it is the Associated Business Machines, a particularly troublesome customer on the Gramercy–7 exchange.

I brought to the job certain radical interests. I knew I would see "bureaucratization," "alienation," and "exploitation." I knew that it was "false consciousness" of their true role in the imperialist economy that led the "workers" to embrace their oppressors. I believed those things and I believe them still. I know why, by my logic, the workers should rise up. But my understanding was making reality an increasing puzzle: Why didn't people move? What things, invisible to me, were holding them back? What I hoped to learn, in short, was something about the texture of the industrial system: what life within it meant to its participants.

I deliberately decided to take a job which was women's work, white collar, highly industrialized and bureaucratic. I knew that New York Tel was in a management crisis notorious both among businessmen and among the public and I wondered what effect the well-publicized breakdown of service was having on employees. Securing the position was not without hurdles. I was "overqualified," having confessed to college; I performed better on personnel tests than I intended to do, and I was inspected for symptoms of militance by a shrewd, but friendly interviewer who noticed the several years' gap in my record of employment. "What have you been doing lately?" she asked me. "Protesting?" I said: "Oh, no, I've been married," as if that condition itself explained one's neglect of social problems. She seemed to agree that it did.

My problem was to talk myself out of a management traineeship at a higher salary while maintaining access to the job I wanted. This, by fabrications, I was able to do. I said: "Well, you see, I'm going through a divorce right now and I'm a little upset emotionally, and I don't know if I want a career with managerial responsibility." She said, "If anyone else said that to me, I'm afraid I wouldn't be able to hire them," but in the end she accepted me. I had the feeling it would have been harder for her to explain to her bosses why she had let me slip away, given my qualifications, than to justify to them her suspicions.

I nonetheless found as I began the job that I was viewed as "management material" and given special treatment. I was welcomed at length by both the District Supervisor and the man who was to be my Manager, and given a set of fluffy feminist speeches about "opportunities for women" at New York Tel. I was told in a variety of ways that I would be smarter than the other people in my class; "management" would be keeping an eye on me. Then the Manager led me personally to the back classroom where my training program was scheduled to begin.

The class consisted of five students and an instructor. Angela and Katherine were two heavy-set Italian women in their late forties. They had been promoted to Commercial after years of employment as clerks in the Repair Department where, as Angela said, "they were expected to be robots." They were unable to make the transition to the heavier demands of the Representative's job and returned to Repair in defeat after about a week.

Billy was a high school boy of seventeen who had somehow been referred by company recruiters into this strange women's world. His lack of adult experience made even simple situations difficult for him to deal with: he could not tell a customer that she had to be in the apartment when an installer was coming without giggling uncontrollably about some imaginary tryst. He best liked "drinking with the boys," a pack of Brooklyn high schoolers whose alcoholism was at the Singapore Sling stage; he must have belonged to one of the last crowds in Brooklyn that had never smoked dope.

Betty was a pretty, overweight, intelligent woman in her mid-twenties who had been a Representative handling "Billing" and was now being "cross-trained" (as they say in the Green Berets) in Orders. She was poised, disciplined, patient, ladylike, competent in class and, to me, somewhat enigmatic outside it: liberal about Blacks, in spite of a segregated high school education, but a virtual Minuteman about Reds, a matter wholly outside her experience. By the end of the class Betty and I had overcome out mutual skepticism enough to be almost friends and if there is anyone at the phone company to whom I feel slightly apologetic—for having listened always with a third ear and for masquerading as what I was not—it is Betty.

Sally, the instructor, was a pleasant, stocky woman in her early thirties with a frosted haircut and eyes made up like a racoon. She had a number of wigs, including one with strange dangling curls. Sally's official role was to persuade us of the rationality of company policies and practices, which she did skillfully and faithfully. In her private life, however, she was a believer in magic, an aficionado rather than a practitioner only because she felt that while she understood how to conjure up the devil, she did not also know how to make him go away. To Sally a disagreeable female customer was not oppressed, wretched, impoverished in her own life, or merely bitchy: she was—literally—a witch. Sally explained to herself by demonology the existence of evils of which she was far too smart to be unaware.

The Representative's course is "programmed." It is apparent that the phone company has spent millions of dollars for high-class management consultation on the best way to train new employees. The two principal criteria are easily deduced. First, the course should be made so routine that any employee can teach it. The teacher's material—the remarks she makes, the examples she uses—are all printed in a loose-leaf notebook that she follows. Anyone can start where anyone else leaves off. I felt that I could teach the course myself, simply by following the program. The second criterion is to assure the reproducibility of results, to guarantee that every part turned out by the system will be <u>interchangeable</u> with every other part. The system is to bureaucracy what Taylor was to the factory: it consists of breaking down every operation into discrete parts, then making verbal the discretions that are made.

At first we worked chiefly from programmed booklets organized around the principle of supplying the answer, then rephrasing the question. For instance:

It is annoying to have the other party to a conversation leave the line without an explanation.
Before leaving, you should excuse yourself and ——— what you are going to do.

Performing skillfully was a matter of reading, and not actual comprehension. Katherine and Angela were in constant difficulty. They "never read," they said. That's why it was hard for them.

Soon acting out the right way to deal with customers became more important than self-instruction. The days were organized into Lesson Plans, a typical early one being: How to Respond to a Customer if You Haven't Already Been Trained to Answer his Question, or a slightly more bureaucratic rendering of that notion. Sally explained the idea, which is that you are supposed to refer the call to a more experienced Representative or to the Supervisor. But somehow they manage to complicate the situation to the point where it becomes confusing even for an intelligent person to handle it. You mustn't say: "Gosh, that's tough, I don't know anything about that, let me give the phone to someone who does," though that in effect is what you do. Instead when the phone rings, you say: "Hello. This is Miss Langer. May I help you?" (The Rule is, get immediate "control of the contact" and hold it lest anything unexpected happen, like, for instance, a human transaction between you and the customer.)

He says: "This is Mr. Smith and I'd like to have an additional wall telephone installed in my kitchen."

You say: "I'll be very glad to help you, Mr. Smith (Rule the Second: Always express interest in the Case and indicate willingness to help), but I'll need more information. What is your telephone number?"

He tells you, then you confess: "Well, Mr. Smith, I'm afraid I haven't been trained in new installations yet because I'm a new representative, but let me give you someone else who can help you." (Rule the Third: You must get his consent to this arrangement. That is, you must say: *May* I get someone else who can help you? *May* I put you on hold for a moment?)

The details are absurd but they are all prescribed. What you would do naturally becomes unnatural when it is codified, and the rigidity of the rules makes the Representatives in training feel they are stupid when they make mistakes. Another lesson, for example, was: What to Do if a Customer Calls and Asks for a Specific Person, such as Miss Smith, another Representative, or the Manager. Whatever the facts, you are to say "Oh, Miss Smith is busy but I have access to your records, may I help you?" A customer is never allowed to identify his interests with any particular employee. During one lesson, however, Sally said to Angela: "Hello, I'd like immediately to speak to Mrs. Brown," and Angela said, naturally, "Hold the line a minute, please. I'll put her on." A cardinal sin, for which she was immediately rebuked. Angela felt terrible.

Company rhetoric asserts that this rigidity does not exist, that Representatives are supposed to use "initiative" and "judgment," to develop their own language. What that means is that instead of using the precise words "Of course I'll be glad to help you but I'll need more information," you are allowed to "create" some individual variant. But you must always (1) express willingness to help and (2) indicate the need for further investigation. In addition, while you are doing this, you must always write down the information taken from the customer, coded, on a yellow form called a CF–1, in such a way as to make it possible for a Representative in Florida to read and translate it. "That's the point," Sally told us. "You are doing it the same way a rep in Illinois or Alaska does it. We're one big monopoly."

The logic of training is to transform the trainees from humans into machines. The basic method is to handle any customer request by extracting "bits" of information: by translating the human problem he might have into bureaucratic language so that it can be processed by the right department. For instance, if a customer calls and says: "My wife is dying and she's coming home from the hospital today and I'd like to have a phone installed in her bedroom right away," you say, "Oh, I'm very sorry to hear that sir, I'm sure I can help you, would you be interested in our Princess model? It has a dial that lights up at night," meanwhile *writing* on your ever-present CF–1: "Csr wnts Prn inst bdrm immed," issuing the order, and placing it in the right-hand side of your work-file where it gets picked up every fifteen minutes by a little clerk.

The knowledge that one is under constant observation (of which more later) I think helps to ensure that contacts are handled in this uniform and wooden manner. If you varied it, and said something spontaneous, you might well be overheard; moreover, it is probably not possible to be especially human when you are concentrating so hard on extracting the bits, and when you have to deal with so many bits in one day.

Sometimes the bits can be extraordinarily complicated. A customer (that is, a CSR) calls and says rapidly, "This is Mrs. Smith and I'm moving from 23rd Street to 68th Street, and I'd like to keep my green Princess phone and add two white Trimlines and get another phone in a metallic finish and my husband wants a new desk phone in his study." You are supposed to have taken that all down as she says it. Naturally you have no time to listen to how she says it, to strike up a conversation, or be friendly. You are desperate to get straight the details.

The dehumanization and the surprising degree of complication are closely related: the number of variables is large, each variable has a code which must be learned and manipulated, and each situation has one—and only one—correct answer. The kind of problem we were taught to handle, in its own language, looks like this:

A CSR has: IMRCV EX CV GRN BCHM IV
He wants: IMRCV WHT EX CV WHT BCHM IV

This case, very simplified, means only that the customer has regular residential phone service with a black phone, a green one, and an ivory bell chime, and that he wants a new service with two white phones and a bell chime. Nonetheless, all these items are charged at differing monthly rates which the Representative must learn where to find and how to calculate: each has a separate installation charge which varies in a number of ways; and, most important, they represent only a few of the dozens of items or services a customer could possibly want (each of which, naturally, has its own rates and variables, its own codes).

He could want a long cord or a short one, a green one or a white one, a new party listed on his line, a special headset for a problem with deafness, a touchtone phone, and on and on and on. For each of the things he could possibly want there would be one and only one correct charge to quote to him, one and only one right way to handle the situation.

It is largely since World War II that the Bell System abandoned being a comparatively simple service organization and began producing such an array of consumer products as to rival Proctor and Gamble. It is important to realize what contribu-

tion this proliferation makes both to creating the work and
making it unbearable. If the company restricted itself to essential functions and services—standard telephones and standard
types of service—whole layers of its bureaucracy would not
need to exist at all, and what did need to exist could be both
more simple and more humane. The pattern of proliferation is
also crucial for among other things, it is largely responsible for
the creation of the "new"—white collar—"working class"
whose job is to process the bureaucratic desiderata of consump-
tion.

In our classroom, the profit motivation behind the telephone
cornucopia is not concealed and we are programmed to repeat
its justifications: that the goods were developed to account for
different "tastes" and the "need of variation." Why Touchtone
Dialing? We learn to say that "it's the latest thing," "it dials
faster," "it is easier to read the letters and numbers," and "its
musical notes as you depress the buttons are pleasant to hear."
We learn that a Trimline is a "space-saver," that it has an "entirely new feature, a recall button that allows you to hang up
without replacing the receiver," and that it is "featured in the
Museum of Modern Art's collection on industrial design." Why
a night-light? we were asked. I consider saying, "It would be
nice to make love by a small sexy light," but instead helped to
contribute the expected answers: "It gives you security in the
bedroom," "it doesn't interfere with the TV."

One day a woman named Carol Nichols, whose job it is to
supervise instruction, came to watch our class. Carol is a typical
telephone company employee: an aging single woman who has
worked her way up to a position of modest authority. In idle
conversation I inquired into the origins of our programmed
instruction. Carol said it was all prepared under centralized
auspices but had recently benefited from the consultation of
two Columbia professors. One, she believed, was the chairman
of the English department; another, an English professor. Their

principal innovation, I gathered, was to suggest formal quizzes in addition to role-playing.

Carol took the content of the work very seriously. She was concerned to impress on us the now familiar Customer's Service Ideology that We Do Help the Customer no matter what his problem. She said: "If the customer tells you to drop dead, you say, 'I'll be very glad to help you sir.'" I couldn't resist raising the obvious question, wondering what is the Rule covering obscene propositions, but saying innocently, "Gee, I can think of things a customer might say that you wouldn't want to help him with." Carol looked very tough and said: "Oh. We don't get *those* kind of calls in the Commercial Department."

Carol threw herself into role-playing tests with gusto. In one of the tests she pretended to be a Mrs. Van Der Pool from Gramercy Park South, whose problem was that she had four dirty white phones that needed cleaning and one gold phone that was tarnishing. Carol enjoyed playing the snotty Mrs. VDP to the hilt, and what sense of identity, projection, or simple resentment went into her characterization it is hard to say. On the other hand, despite her caricatured and bossy airs, Carol was very nice to the women in the class. At the end, when Angela and Katherine were complaining that they were doing so poorly, Carol gave them a little pep talk in which she said that she had been miserable on her first day as a Rep, had cried, but had just made up her mind to get through it, and had been able to do so.

"Many have passed this way and they all felt the way you do," she told them. "Just keep at it. You can do it." Angela and Katherine were very grateful to Carol for this. Later in the week when frustrated and miserable, Katherine broke down and cried. Sally too was unobtrusive, sympathetic, encouraging.

Selling is an important part of the Representative's job. Sally introduced the subject with a little speech (from her program book) about the concept of the "well telephoned home," how that was an advance from the old days when people thought of telephone equipment in a merely functional way. Now, she said, we stress "a variety of items of beauty and convenience." Millions of dollars have been spent by the Bell System she told us, to find out what a customer wants and to sell it to him. She honestly believed that good selling is as important to the customer as it is to the company: to the company because "it makes additional and worthwhile revenue," to the customer because it provides services that are truly useful. We are warned not to attempt to sell when it is clearly inappropriate to do so, but basically to use every opportunity to unload profitable items. This means that if a girl calls up and asks for a new listing for a roommate, your job is to say: "Oh. Wouldn't your roommate prefer to have her own extension?"

The official method is to avoid giving the customer a choice but to offer him a total package which he can either accept or reject. For instance, a customer calls for new service. You find out that he has a wife, a teenage daughter, and a six-room apartment. The prescription calls for you to get off the line, make all the calculations, then come back on and say all at once: "Mr. Smith, suppose we installed for you a wall telephone in your kitchen, a Princess extension in your daughter's room and one in your bedroom, and our new Trimline model in your living room. This will cost you only X dollars for the installation and only Y dollars a month."

Mr. Smith will say, naturally, "That's too many telephones for a six-room apartment," and you are supposed to "overcome his objections" by pointing out the "security" and "convenience" that comes from having telephones all over the place.

Every Representative is assigned a selling quota—so many extensions, so many Princesses—deduced and derived in some way from the quota of the next largest unit. In other words, quotas are assigned to the individual because they are first assigned to the five-girl unit; they are assigned to the unit because they are assigned to the twenty-girl section; and they are assigned to the section because they are assigned to the district: to the manager and the district supervisor. The fact that everyone is in the same situation—expected to contribute to the same total—is one of the factors that increase management-worker solidarity.

The women enact the sales ritual as if it were in fact in their own interest and originated with them. Every month there is a sales contest. Management provides the money—$25.00 a month to one or another five-girl unit—but the women do the work: organizing skits, buying presents, or providing coffee and donuts to reward the high sellers. At Thanksgiving the company raffled away turkeys: the number of chances one had depended on the number of sales one had completed.

As the weeks passed our training grew more and more rigid. For each new subject we followed an identical Army-like ritual beginning with "Understanding the Objectives" and ending with "Learning the Negotiation." The Objectives of the "Lesson on Termination of Service," for instance, were:

1. To recognize situations where it is appropriate to encourage users to retain service.
2. To be able to apply Save effort successfully.
3. To negotiate orders for Termination.
4. To offer "Easy Move."
5. To write Termination orders.

Or, for example, Cords. It is hard to believe such a subject could be complicated but in fact it is: cords come in different sizes, standard and special, and have different costs, different colors, and different installation intervals. There is also the weighty matter of the distinction between the handset cord (connecting the receiver to the base) and the mounting cord (connecting the base to the wall or floor). The ritual we were taught to follow when on the telephone with a customer goes like this, and set up on our drawing board it looked like this as well:

*Fact-finding:*
1. Business or residence.
2. New or existing service.
3. Reason for request
   a. handset or mounting cord
   b. approximate length
4. Type of set or location.
5. Other instruments in the household and where located.
6. Customer's phone number.

Then you get:

*Off the line* where you
1. Get Customer's records.
2. Think and Plan What to Do.
3. Check reference materials.
4. Check with supervisor if necessary.

Then you return to the line with a:

*Recommendation:*
1. Set stage for recommendation.
2. Suggest alternative where appropriate or
3. Accept order for cord.
4. Suggest appropriate length.
   a. Verify handset or mounting
5. Present recommendation for suitable equipment that "goes with" request including monthly rental (for instance an extension bell).
6. Determine type of instrument and color.
7. Quote total non-recurring charges.
8. Arrange appointment date. Access to the Apartment, and Whom to See.

On the floor, substantial departure from this ritual is an Error (more later). This pattern of learning became so intolerable that, one day, while waiting for Sally to return from lunch, the class invented a lesson of its own. We called it Erroneous Disconnections. The Objectives were:

1. To identify situations in which it is appropriate to disconnect Customer.

2. To apply the necessary techniques so that disconnects can be accomplished with minimum irritation to the Representative.

3. To accomplish these ends without being observed.

We then identified a variety of situations in which our natural response would be to disconnect. I was surprised by how deeply Billy and Betty were caught up in our parody, and I thought it represented an ability to dissociate from the company which most of the time was very little in evidence; it seemed to me somehow healthy and promising.

*Disc.*

As the weeks wore on our classes became in some ways more bizarre. On several afternoons we were simultaneously possessed by the feeling that we simply couldn't bear it and—subtly at first but with increasing aggression as time passed—we would simply stop work: refuse to learn any more. At these times all kinds of random discussions would take place. On one occasion we spent an entire afternoon discussing the Seven Wonders of the Ancient World and calling up information services of newspapers to find out what they were; on another afternoon Sally explained at great length her views on magic.

At first I believed that these little work stoppages were spontaneous but later, as we completed our class work close to schedule, I came to believe that this was not so: that they were a part of our program and were meant to serve as an opportunity for the instructor to discover any random things about our views and attitudes the company might find useful to know. In any event, partly because of these chats and partly because of the intensity of our training experience, by the end of the class we were a fairly solid little unit. We celebrated our graduation with perfume for Sally, a slightly alcoholic and costly lunch, and great good feeling all around.

Observers at the phone company. They are everywhere. I became aware of a new layer of Observation every day. The system works like this. For every five or six women there is, as

I have said, a Supervisor who can at any moment listen in from the phone set on her desk to any of her Representatives' contacts with a customer. For an hour every day, the Supervisor goes to a private room off the main floor where she can listen (herself unobserved) to the conversations of any of her "girls" she chooses. The women know, naturally, *when* she is doing this but not *whose* contact she is observing.

Further off the main floor is a still more secret Observing Room staffed by women whose title and function is, specifically, Observer. These women "jack in" at random to any contact between any Representative and a customer: their job is basically to make sure that the Representatives are giving out correct information. Furthermore, these observers are themselves observed from a central telephone company location elsewhere in the city to make sure that they are not reporting as incorrect information which is actually correct. In addition the Observers make "access calls" by which they check to see that the telephone lines are open for the customers to make their connections. This entire structure of observation is, of course, apart from the formal representative-supervisor-manager-district supervisor-division-head chain of managerial command. They are, in effect, parallel hierarchical structure.

One result of the constant observation (the technology being unbounded) is that one can never be certain where the observation stops. It is company policy to stress its finite character, but no one ever knows for sure. Officials of the Communications Workers of America have testified, for instance, that the company over-indulged in the wired-Martini stage of technology, bugging the pen sets of many of its top personnel. At ———— Street there were TV cameras in the lobby and on the elevators. This system coexists with the most righteous official attitude toward wiretapping. Only supervisors and managers can deal with wiretap complaints; Federal regulations about the sanctity of communications are posted; and the overt position toward taps, in the lower managerial echelons, is that they are simply illegal and, if they exist, must be the result of private entrepreneurship (businesses bugging one another) rather than Government policy.

"If someone complains about a tap," Sally said, "I just ask them: Why would anyone be tapping your phone?" Consciousness of the Government's "internal security" net is simply blacked out. Nonetheless, the constant awareness of the company's ability to observe creates unease: Are the lounge phones wired into the Observing structure? Does the company tap the phones of new or suspicious personnel? Is union activity monitored? No one can say with confidence.

Sally had two voices, one human, one machine, and in her machine voice on the very first day she explained the justification for Observation. "The thing about the phone company," she said, "is that it has No Product except the Service it Gives. If this were General Motors we would know how to see if we were doing a good job: we could take the car apart and inspect the parts and see that they were all right and that it was well put together. But at the phone company we can't do that. All we can do is check ourselves to see that we are doing a good job."

She took the same attitude toward "access calls," explaining that a completed access call is desirable because it indicates to the manager and everyone up the line that the wires are open and the system is working as it should. The position toward Observers she attempted to inculcate was one of gratitude: Observers are good for you. They help you measure your job and see if you are doing well.

The system of Observers is linked with the telephone company's ultimate weapon, the Service Index by which Errors are charted and separate units of the company rated against each other. Throughout training—in class and in our days on the floor —hints of the monumental importance of the Index in the psychic life of the employees continually emerged. "Do you know how many Errors you're allowed?" Sally would ask us. "No Errors"—proud that the standard was so high. Or: "I can't afford an Error"—from my supervisor, Laura, on the floor, explaining why she was keeping me roped in on my first days on the job. But the system was not revealed in all its parts until the very end of training when as a *pièce de resistance* the manager, Y, came in to give a little talk billed as a discussion of "Service" but in fact an attempt to persuade the class of the logic of observation.

Y was a brooding, reserved man in his mid-twenties, a kind of Ivy League leftover who looked as if he'd accidentally got caught in the wrong decade. His talk was very much like Sally's. "We need some way to measure Service. If a customer doesn't like Thom McCann shoes he can go out and buy Buster Brown. Thom McCann will know something is wrong. But the phone company is a monopoly, people can't escape it, they have no other choice. How can we tell if our product, Service, is good?" He said that observation was begun in 1924 and that, although the Company had tried other methods of measuring service, none had proved equally satisfactory. Specifically, he said, other methods failed to provide an accurate measure of the work performance of one unit as opposed to another.

Y's was a particularly subtle little speech. He used the Socratic method always asking us to give the answers or formulate the rationales, always asking is it right? Is it fair? (I'm certain that if we did not agree it was right and fair, he wanted to know.) He stressed the limited character of observation. His units (twenty "girls"), he said, took about 10,000 calls per month; of these only 100 were observed, or about five observations per woman per month. He emphasized that these checks were random and anonymous. He explained that the Index has four components which govern what the observers look for:

Contact Performance Defects (CPD)
Customer Waiting Interval (CWI)

Contacts Not Closed (CNC)
Business Office Accessibility (BOA)
The CPD is worth 70 percent of the Index, the other factors 10 percent each. The elements of CPD are, for example, incomplete or incorrect information, making inadequate arrangements, or mistreating a customer; the elements of BOA are the amount of time it takes a customer to reach the central switchboard, and the promptness of the Representative in answering the phone after the connection has been made. Points are assigned on a scientific basis, based on the number of errors caught by the observers. Charts are issued monthly, rating identical units of the company against each other. Y's unit (mine) was the top unit in Manhattan, having run for the preceeding three months or so at about 97 or 98 percent. While I was there there was a little celebration, attended by high company officials, in which Y was awarded a plaque and the women on the floor given free "coffee and danish."

Now, a number of things about this system are obvious. First, demeaning and demanding as it is, it clearly provides management with information it believes it has a desperate need to know. For instance, there was a unit on the East Side of Manhattan running at about an 85 percent level. The mathematics of it are complicated but it basically means that about 12,000 people every month were getting screwed by the department in one form or another: they asked for a green phone and the Representative ordered a black one; they arranged to be home on the 24th and the woman told the installer to come on the 25th; they were told their service would cost $10.00 and it actually cost $25.00, and so forth. Management has to know which of its aspirants scrambling up the ladder to reward and which to punish.

On the other hand, their official justifications for observation are a lie for two reasons. First, the Index does not measure actual service: our unit could run at 98 percent while half the phones in our area were out of service because the Index does not deal with the service departments of the company which are, in fact, where its troubles are. The angriest customer in Manhattan would not show up as an error on the Index if he were treated politely and his call transferred: the Commercial Index is a chimera capable of measuring only its internal functioning, and that functioning, being simply bureaucratic, is cut off from the real world of telephone service and servicing. Secondly, it is a lie because it does not spring from the root that management claims—that is, the absence of a tangible physical product (observation is in fact commonplace in industry where the nonexistence of a product is not an issue) but from another root: the need to control behavior. That is, if the system is technically linked to measurement of service it is functionally linked to control.

Furthermore, it works: it absolutely controls behavior. On December 24, the one day of the year when there is no observation (and no contribution to the Index) the concept of service utterly disappeared. The women mistreated the customers and told them whatever came into their minds. Wall lights whose flickering on a normal day indicates that customers are receiving busy signals were flashing wildly: no one cared about the BOA.

But on a normal day, the Index is King. It is a rule, for instance, that if one Representative takes over a call for another, the first must introduce the second to the customer, saying "Sir, I'm going to put Miss Laramie on the line. She'll be able to help you." "Don't forget to introduce me," said Miss L. anxiously to me one day. "An observer might be listening." Or: we were repeatedly told *never* to check the box labeled "Missed on Regular Delivery" on the form authorizing delivery of directories. ("It will look as if Commercial made an Error," Sally told us, "when the Error is really Directory's.) This awareness of observers and Errors is constant not because of fear of individ-

ual reprisal—there is none—but because of block loyalty: first
to the immediate unit of five women, then to the twenty-
women unit, then to the still larger office.

The constant weighing, checking, competition, also binds the
managers to the women and is another source of the over-
whelmingly paternalistic atmosphere: the managers are only as
good as their staffs and they are rated by the same machine. The
women make, or don't make, the Errors; the managers get, or
don't get, the plaques and the promotions.

What the system adds up to is this : if we count both supervisors and observers, at least three people are responsible for the
correct performance of any job, and that is because the system
is based on hiring at the lowest level, keeping intelligence suppressed, and channeling it into idiotic paths. The process is
circular: hire women who are not too talented (for reasons of
social class, limited educational opportunities, etc.); suppress
them even further by the "scientific" division of the job into
banal components which defy initiative or the exercise of intelligence; then keep them down by the institutionalization of
pressures and spies.

Surely it would be better if the jobs' horizons were broadened
—a reformist goal—the women were encouraged to take initiative and responsibility, and then left on their own. And it would
be better yet if those aspects of the work directly tied to the
company's profit-oriented and "capitalistic" functions—the
Princess and Trimline phones and all the bureaucratic complications that stem from their existence—were eliminated altogether and a socialized company concentrated on providing
all the people with uniform and decent service. But—

# 6

# THE CLASS STRUGGLE:
## Death and Transfiguration at Caltex

### Serge Mallet

In 1931 Texaco established an oil refinery at Ambès, a small
village near Bordeaux at the confluence of the Dordogne and
Garonne rivers. Serge Mallet spent nine months there in 1958,
studying the work patterns of the refinery and talking with its
employees. The essay which came from this experience was
published, along with accounts of his visits to other companies,
in a volume entitled *The New Working Class*.

This essay struck my eye because it shows how close is the
relationship between the nature of work, the relationship of the
individual worker to the company, and the workers' general
attitudes toward class movements and political power. Unlike
the auto assemblers at Renault, the refinery workers at Ambès
appear little interested in explosive political questions, or at
least in using their local organizations to participate in nationwide political campaigns. Their primary concern appears to be
some sort of worker control over their own enterprise. I have
helped argue elsewhere (Edward Shorter and Charles Tilly,
*Strikes in France*) that the kind of work men do may predispose

SOURCE: Serge Mallet, *La Nouvelle classe ouvrière* (Paris: Editions du Seuil,
1963), pp. 146–175. Reprinted with permission of the publisher. My translation.

them to one sort of political concern or another, to participation in "revolutionary" movements for the seizure of power at the center of the nation-state, or to shop-control movements within local settings. I am unable to document or even to fully illustrate that case within a volume of this scope. But I at least alert the reader to it, for this is the sole selection in the book which builds firm bridges between industrial technology and more general political concerns.

Mallet is currently undertaking research within the Laboratory for the Sociology of Knowledge in Paris, and is active in French politics.

## The Workers

The key to understanding the refinery is the continuousness of its operations. From where the raw oil enters through huge reserve tanks, to the topping unit, to the many parts of the system responsible for the many kinds of end products, all operations are conducted in a smooth, uninterrupted flow. The heart of this great arterial system is the high-pressure steam center, activated by waste gases from the refining process, which drives the turbines and alternators, which, in turn, propel about the crude oil.

Within this system an almost total degree of automation prevails. Because no manual operations are involved, and because the processing of the oil is continuous, the essential duty of the refinery workers is the control of the various pressures, temperatures, and rates of flow. Because the physical and chemical reactions always take place within very fine tolerances, any discontinuity in the flow of the oil or variance in the temperature would entail disastrous consequences, possibly an explosion, certainly the severe impairment of the product's quality and the installation's operation. In the modern units for reforming, cracking, and polymerizing, temperatures are extremely high and the chemical reactions very rapid; the risk of catas-trophe is manifestly increased. The human eye and hand are inadequate here as rigorous instruments of control and supervi-sion. All the technicians say it would be completely impossible to function without automation.

A team of three workers is sufficient to run an entire unit within the refinery. Changing shifts every eight hours (for the refinery operates night and day), a team is composed of a chief operator, a control-panel monitor, and an assistant or pump attendant. The chief operator, who performs in the automated plant the old master craftsman's role, is responsible for his two teammates, supervises their work, makes his surveillance rounds, takes care of liaison with the units located before and after his own in the productive process, and works with the maintenance personnel should repair work be needed. As the man responsible for his unit, he must of course know intimately its functioning, the nature and preconditions of the chemical reactions taking place, and the interpretation of the control gauges. He is, moreover, classified in the category of "staff."

The man who monitors the controls runs the actual operation of the unit. Electronic devices perform automatically the ad-justments of the equipment, and so his role consists mainly in making sure the automated controls always function properly. But precisely this sort of supervision demands, it goes without saying, a knowledge of the processes being performed, as well as of the servomechanisms doing the regulating. He must spot immediately on his control board any unexpected readings, such as might come from abnormal chemical reactions or from the defective performance of the control instruments.

Finally, the pump attendant is the only member of the team actually to get his hands dirty, a man whose function is similar to that of a regular worker's. He takes care of the operation of the pumps, the heating equipment, and the compressors. He draws off samples for analysis, changes such smooth-flow parts as the burners, and makes sure fuel supplies are adequate.

The control personnel in total—that is, the people who operate the refinery—is scarcely more than fifty men. This workforce has direct responsibility for an annual production of between 1 and 4 million tons of petroleum products.

Thus a human dimension is involved, despite the fact that an oil refinery precisely evokes the compelling image of the "factory without workers," despite the Martian landscape of high towers, giant reservoirs, and endless labyrinths of pipe in which these surrealistic creatures seem lost. Nor could the refinery function without a second group of people, the maintenance workers.

The various refinery installations are constantly subject to all kinds of enormous pressures. Wear and tear is especially hard on the plant's true arterial system, the pipe networks and control valves which haul daily thousands of tons of various products. Neither the pumps and turbines nor the furnaces and other components of the production units hold out indefinitely. There is, of course, nowadays a tendency to use increasingly resistant metals and alloys, and productive units which some years ago had to shut down every three months for inspection now function almost everywhere for an entire year without interruption. But it is at the price of constant surveillance, the job of the maintenance staff. Composed of mechanics, pipemen, and instrument repairmen, maintenance teams are attached to each unit of production, while mobile crews traverse the whole refinery. The maintenance service does not stop at replacing defective parts or restoring to service "tired" installations: maintenance also means periodically cleaning the equipment as well. It is maintenance which makes equipment adjustments for new productive cycles, called into being by changing demand, or for processing new kinds of crude oil with a different organic composition. Clearly, the workers in these teams are both highly and narrowly specialized. Working conditions in the refineries impose a very rigorous discipline, the place of each man being strictly determined. A maintenance worker can't take a simple broom to clean the slake off pipes; he must know how to use the cleaning machine. Maintenance crews—recruited from among highly skilled workers in machine building, electronics, or watchmaking—enjoy, as do the operators, full and complete responsibility within the limits of their jobs. Their working conditions are more similar to those of former artisans than those of workers in the machine-assembling industries whence many of them came.

## The Work and Authority Relationships

In an industrial sector where individual "machines" do not exist and where, quite to the contrary, profitability is based on the continuous operation of the installation as a whole, the responsibility which each worker enjoys creates "optimum psychological conditions," permitting each man to perform his task effectively. Either as operative or as maintenance man, the worker is master of his job. He carrys out a function within the framework of which he is the sole judge of his own decisions. Alone or almost alone at his post, he bears full responsibility for what he does. No one can arbitrarily intervene in his sphere, and the engineers are often called back into line when they infringe upon this strict division of labor.

The management of Caltex has moreover introduced a job classification system which "theorizes" this preoccupation with job control through a sort of hierarchical notation system. But it is practically impossible to actually quantify the importance of the privilege. Older workers recruited from the peasantry were concerned mainly with the physical arduousness and salubriousness of a job, as well as with the material benefits it brought them. But former *factory* workers at Caltex, who have experienced the degrading routine of mechanization, the robotry of the assembly line, and the withering ossification of the human mind, appreciate fully this "rehabilitation of work."

This appreciation goes hand in hand with the workers' attitude toward management. In the old mills with their assembly lines, militancy was almost always violent. It was more an explosion of rage than an organized movement, and all union organizers know well the notion of "temperature." The temperature of the shop might well have been at the boiling point, even in the absence of some particular grievance which would have justified a strike at that moment: if the temperature were right, the strike would nonetheless take off. If, however, the temperature were not hot enough, even the best elaborated and most justified demands had no chance of drawing support from the rank and file. When a strike did break out, it took on a cast of revolutionary violence, frequently progressing to vandalism and machine breaking. More than a political act, such a strike was an affirmation of individual identity. By refusing to play along, the worker showed he was still a human being. By stopping the machines which controlled his daily life patterns, he created the illusion of controlling his own destiny. The strike was the dialectical negation of the dehumanization of work.

At Caltex, nothing of the kind happens. Although working conditions do more than high wages to relax the climate of authority here, it would be false to speak of "an absence of class consciousness." On the contrary, relationships between workers and management are marked by an extraordinary self-awareness. The all-powerful union is highly respected, and management has virtually given up going over its head—which would be relatively simple in an operation of five hundred workers, all of whom are more or less dispersed. It is fairer to talk of "peaceful coexistence" between the two camps and all that entails by way of tension, conflict, and permanent rivalries, but also by way of fair play in the contest.

We are in the presence here of a unique phenomenon, at least for France. And precisely because the refinery is a sort of virgin soil, we can see that outside influences have contributed very little to forming this frame of mind. The work force of the refinery consists of 560 workers and staff . . . almost equally divided among the three services of office work, maintenance, and operations. The maintenance workers come mainly from factories in Bordeaux, although a certain number of them, notably the laborers and the unskilled, stem from peasant families in the Bourgeais and the Entre-deux-Mers [nearby farming regions], men who, having worked on the construction of the new refinery, have become "integrated" into its permanent work force.

The operating crews have a more complex social composition. About half of their members come from cities, principally Bordeaux, and have quite varied backgrounds. Former barbers, university dropouts, bankrupt small merchants, craftsmen from the artisanal sector, all have been molten together in a new occupation where former professional skills count for little. The other half of the operators have been recruited from the local neighborhood, the sons of small peasant proprietors on the other bank of the river.

In the early years vast differences appeared among the mentalities of these various kinds of workers. Whereas the Bordeaux workers carried into the refinery their traditional proletarian attitudes, with all that means in terms of detachment from the enterprise, the peasants distinguished themselves by their zeal and their servility. Being a worker was for many of them only a temporary condition. Indeed there were many peasant small holders who hired someone else to run their vineyards while they worked at good pay in the refinery. Each hour of overtime represented for these men the chance to buy another little parcel of ground, to get a sorely needed horse or tractor, to do over the roof of their storehouse or fix up the wine cellar.

But this situation, classic since the French working class began to form itself from such peasant groups in the 1840s, lasted scarcely a year or two. In a single crop region devoted to viticulture, farmers are exposed precariously to climatic hazards and highly competitive market conditons. So all the other one-time peasants, seduced by the material security Caltex offered, began to withdraw themselves from their vineyards. Training on the job brought a rapid transformation in the peasant's former cultural world. The work rhythms of machine industry are poorly suited to the countryman's habits. But work at the refinery was different, demanding considerable reflection on the part of the personnel, an acute awareness of one's technical responsibilities, a certain familiarity with the logic behind the productive process—all qualities quite similar to those needed by vintners, the artisans of agriculture. So adaptation for these peasants was easy.

The transformation of group psychologies took longer. But management's concern with "integration" led, after 1950, to intensive training programs. The adoption of suggestion boxes, the free loan of technical books, the publication of "France-Caltex," a plant newspaper full of readable material, and above all the sending of young men in the operating service as apprentices to other European Caltex refineries and even to the United States, all contributed very quickly to breaking old allegiances among the work force. One can with little difficulty imagine what upheaval for some young peasant, whose horizons had not exceeded the local county seat, a three-or six-month trip to some great German or Italian refinery might provoke, or indeed a voyage to the shores of the Pacific!

This process of adaptation permitted the Caltex management to form a stable work force, technically advanced, and tied by a thousand bonds to a company which had enlarged men's horizons and improved remarkably their living conditions.

Phenomena such as absenteeism, leaving one's post, and alcoholism—all classic vices of a work force of rural origin—rapidly disappeared at Caltex. But the quest for overtime hours, the excess of zeal, and the rejection of worker solidarity and union traditions followed this routing out of peasant mentalities.

Thus within a few years was constructed an autonomous, homogeneous, industrial enterprise. The curious nature of the work, the uniqueness of the recruitment of the workers, the refinery's relative isolation from the big city of Bordeaux, all would ineluctably evoke a new style of labor force, one taking quite different stances than would a big-city proletariat to social issues. . . .

## A New Kind of Industrial Conflict

Wage increases at Caltex resulted mainly from aggressive action on the part of the workers themselves, rather than from management's goodwill. Between 1955 and 1957 the melting pot at Ambès began to solidify. New hiring stopped, as did resignations. The peasant labor force accepted its new worker status, and the former workers from Bordeaux settled into the plant as well. The office staff crystallized in form with the introduction of IBM computers.

This integration, desired, greeted, and abetted by management, ended in reinforcing the union. Whereas five years earlier, workers considered as union organizers were fired, today the unions—and especially the majoritarian CGT [a Communist union confederation]—control even hiring. The union has the first right of suggesting new men for vacant posts. "Confidence" placed in the union means the hiring will be done responsibly, and the adaptation of the new employee to the spirit of the firm is in this manner accelerated. At the same time, this hiring arrangement confers upon the union enormous power, comparable to that enjoyed by the huge American unions within their gigantic firms.

The nature of relationships between management and the union may be seen in the story of a strike. When in March 1957 the union leaders, after some consultation, ordered a walkout, they knew perfectly well that the company could not possibly hold out against them. Moreover, as a courtesy they took measures to safeguard the security of the equipment. The maintenance staff stopped work but stood by ready to intervene in case of an accident; and the operating service merely slowed down the pace of processing rather than halting it entirely. There was not in fact a work stoppage, but rather a lowering of pressure resulting in a lessening of output. Tankers were even unloaded during the strike.

A complete work stoppage of several weeks, entailing the shutdown of the plant and perhaps some damage to the equipment, weighed upon the minds of both union and management negotiators. As long as negotiations were underway, the unions kept secret, at the explicit request of management, word that a strike was in progress. Thus no commercial consequences were suffered, such as the rerouting of tankers toward other refineries, which news of the strike would surely have provoked. Three days later management gave in to all worker demands: to a general pay increase of 15 percent and to the readjustment of individual wages sometimes up to 90 percent, more overtime, social benefits, and so forth. The board of directors made the head of personnel responsible for the strike, which cost the petroleum combine tens of millions of francs in three days. The days lost on strike were paid, a logical concession because work had never ceased entirely and the workers had never, in any way, abandoned their posts. Union power emerged stronger than ever from this sensational victory. At this writing [1958], almost all the refinery workers are unionized, a phenomenon which deserves some reflection.

Thus we have had the chance to study close-up the formation of group consciousness within this homogeneous cluster of workers, thrown together within the refinery from among so many different elements. Numerous other studies have examined the formation of an agrarian work force slammed into factory work. The complete absence of collective awareness, the absolute ignorance of even the most elementary rights, the lack of interest in the workings of the shop, all go hand in hand with the brutal rhythms of mechanical work. We have witnessed here the completely opposite development. At the beginning, skilled workers constituted an infinitesimal minority of the labor force; moreover, the new conditions in which they found themselves made useless a large part of their craft skills; it was necessary for these men, as for others, to do a new apprenticeship in the complex operations of the refinery.

### Class Consciousness in an "Integrated" Enterprise

The geographical location of the refinery tends to isolate it from the rest of the working class. The singular nature of the industry and the problems it poses discourage the formation of district or nationwide unions. At the Labor Exchange in Bordeaux, the oil workers are considered as "different": ducks amidst the brood of proletarian chickens.

The refinery offers its employees working conditions much better those in the region as a whole, an area hallmarked by economic underdevelopment and by the dispersal of industrial activity in small artisanal shops, possessing neither foreign markets nor a nationwide clientele. The oil industry's very nature assures workers job security; its technical characteristics signify work that is light and clean.

Thus, the merest flickerings of class struggle would seem unlikely. Now it happens that class consciousness—by which we mean the awareness of a permanent conflict of interest opposing employers and workers—is *more* developed at the refinery than elsewhere. Here unions exert an influence such as they seldom have in other plants.

Precisely because they have learned the importance both of their own productive functions and of the enterprise's role within the economy as a whole, the oil workers at Ambès are aware of their power. Precisely because they have learned they can make management submit in a showdown, they are able to resist the seductive nonsense of Caltex's paternalism. And management itself is quite anonymous. The manager of the refinery and the general director of the European subsidiary are, for the workers, quite separate from the mysterious agents of bankers higher up in New York or San Francisco who run the oil industry. Monsieur Boussac, the local director, is still a real man, whom one sees from time to time in the plant, or more frequently on the front pages of the weekly tabloid, but who is Monsieur Caltex?

The depersonalization of ownership works in two ways: the worker no longer feels any emotional attachment to these nameless phantoms nor is he able to hate them. Thus sentimental notions vanish from class awareness. It becomes only the cold methodical expression of a certain kind of juridical relationship within the productive machinery. In the old champagne firm, which for a century represented the only industrial establishment of the nearby small town, the workers hated the owner but were willing to accept starvation wages. At Ambès the workers neither know who the employer is nor care. But that is only one aspect of the question.

The workers' inability to associate a name, a human symbol of any kind, with the ownership of the refinery marches hand in hand with a very clear awareness of the ties which bind them to the company: occupational ties, social ties, ties of prosperity. They learned their jobs in the refinery, they learned how the world of work runs in the refinery, and the refinery gives many material advantages which, in the case of sudden death, severe illness or disability, or indeed of old age, will prolong their future security far beyond the years in which they do productive work. Thus the notion of this living, indestructible "contract" with Caltex causes them to preoccupy themselves in a surprisingly acute way with the financial operation of the enterprise. The employee representatives to the works' council subject the company's books to a scrutiny just as intense as that of the most conscientious stockholders. Caltex's management, of course, rubs its hands in glee when the union decides to give wage increase demands a backseat to the company's new investment requirements. But management becomes more uneasy when the workers, accepting at face value the rigged balance sheet of the French subsidiary, express concern over disadvantageous marketing arrangements and, indeed, have the audacity to challenge pricing policies and to suggest development programs.

This interest is not confined to the union leaders. For the most part, mimeographed reports of the meeting of the central works' council are studied intently by the worker themselves. Financial policies of the enterprise are discussed and challenged. The workers are astonished at how much it costs to service debts and how much to purchase raw materials. To be sure, we are dealing with a phenomenon just in the making. The time has not yet arrived for the sons of local vintners to have an exact notion of what "worker control" involves. Nor do they have much of a sense of the extraordinary complexity of the productive mechanisms in which they are involved.


## Company and Class

It was fundamentally these questions that I wanted to take up with the union leaders at Ambès. For these men, militant members of the national CGT or former members of the Communist party, feel themselves confronted, in their isolation, with difficult questions.

All admit that it's impossible for them to launch movements with the general slogans of their national organization. On their own, they have come to a certain understanding of the class struggle and of the union's role which depends upon this first premise: that they are tied to the life of the refinery. And in any event, their struggles take place *within* this entity. One might almost say that they consider their relationships with the "boss" as a family affair, taken into the bargain, of course, that this is an impersonal family in which emotionality plays no role. This realization bothers them. For although this union has permitted not a trace of flagging in its combativeness, although it has not shown the slightest tendency toward "sweetheart" arrangements with management, and although it is the massive incarnation of the unified bloc of workers against management (unlike those unions in, say, the automobile industry, where shouting matches and demagogic inflation of rhetoric have lost all following among the workforce), the fact nonetheless remains that in reality, if not in theory, class solidarity has been broken. The mass meetings of metalworkers from plants along the Garonne—where bolts fly against the helmets of the state security police, the violent strike meetings invariably terminated by shamefaced returns to work—seem at the refinery to belong to another world.

"Our problems are different," say the leaders. To be sure, but haven't you gentlemen still broken all solidarity ties with the proletariat you belong to? Do you not, in fact, resign yourselves to capitalism once you have made sure that every man among you has fuel for his fireplace, certainty of work, and security for his old age? After all, that would be only natural. And why in heaven, in view of the fact that the revolutionary CGT is the majority union, did a 1958 attempt by some salaried employees to form a "house union" have such pathetic results?

In this union headquarters, built solidly of chiseled stone and illuminated by cheerful reflections from the river of the night-lights at the refinery, we have the painful impression of having seen the future of the worker movement in Western society. Because there is not a shadow of a doubt that the petrochemical firms, which in the next three or four years are going to be established at the confluence of these two rivers, will resemble far more the science fiction architecture of the refinery than the dark saw-teeth of the machine-works along the Garonne. That the problems we have touched on will be those of French industry of tomorrow.

"The atomization of union structure," an apparently minor consequence of the structural transformations of French industry, lays bare the following dangerous development: because productive work in the most advanced industries such as petroleum, chemicals, electronics, and certain areas of metallurgy, has little in common with either traditional mechanized industry, where Taylorism continues to be the rule, or with small-shop manufacturing, where tens of thousands of workers are still employed, there can be little genuine solidarity among the workers of these different sectors. Only in the huge civil service bureaucracies, characterized by a uniformity of working conditions and employment status, can there still be the true notion of worker solidarity. But there are still further consequences.

## The Depoliticalization of the Unions

The working class never moves directly from class consciousness, as expressed in plant-level militancy, to revolutionary consciousness, to an awareness of the need to change the legal basis of the system of production. This evolution normally takes place via the whirlpool of strike militancy, and it is the direct intervention of the state on behalf of the employers which makes the workers challenge directly the existence of the state. Violence serves in such cases as a school for revolutionaries. But now, just as the basic modes of production change, the manner shifts as well in which the capitalist class uses the state.

The state can get by with using force as long as the workers are an unstable and replaceable "floating mass." *But in the automated factory force, this is absolutely unthinkable.* The development of revolutionary consciousness becomes more complicated. The worker in the automated factory lives in the vicinity of the plant and is almost never driven into conflict with the bourgeois state, save over questions of economic interest. Inevitably such workers shy away from any explicit statement of conflict, especially when the reasons and the forces for such conflict are unclear to them. Hence the success of the slogan: "Keep politics out of the union."

But at the same time, the worker's ever increasing integration into the productive mechanism leads him just as inevitably to go beyond "porkchop" demands in labor struggles and to start thinking about his role in the control of the industrial plant. The very conditions in which he works, by reinforcing his sense of the individual responsibility of the productive artisan, further this process of shop-floor consciousness, just as artisans in small towns and villages in preindustrial society became the most active participants in politics.

*cf. chapt 3, above.*

## Shop-Floor Participation and Worker Control

It is in this way, and this way only, that labor militancy in the technologically most advanced industries can turn into a struggle for socialism, a struggle for a "free society of producers." It is also in this way that, for the first time in history, the struggle for job control will spread beyond the workers as such to the technicians and management personnel of the industrial system, a logical extension of a technological evolution.

The old dogmatic distinction between the "political struggle" and the "economic struggle," which in practice means using minor demands to launch large-scale collective movements for political and parliamentary objectives, becomes meaningless here.

Instead, the union's use of the few controls over plant administration it has already acquired, combined with the pressure points the industrial plant offers by its very nature, suggest a new form of worker militancy. It is a form which, with every

new day, enlarges a bit more the proletariat's real participation
in the apparatus of business administration, and which exposes
ever more the internal contradictions between the legal ownership of the means of production and the social reality of work.
It goes without saying that such a form of militancy, already
transforming in various subtle ways the nature of American
unionism, can only affect a small minority of the French working class. And there is a risk that the new unionism will be
sidetracked from its revolutionary potential by the relative isolation of the only categories of workers capable of promoting it.

But an even greater risk is that the worker movement will
end up the captive of the *most backward segments of the working class,* those in marginal enterprises and in plants of relative
unimportance to the nation's industrial life, if it does not hence-
forth mobilize all of its theoretical, political, financial, and cultural resources for the task of training new leaders for the new
struggle, men who will have nothing in common with the organizers of the "heroic era."

If it does not shift to the workers in these new high technology industries, the worker movement will become a mere
shock troop, compelled to make alliances with the forces of
political reaction.

# SELECT BIBLIOGRAPHY

## The History of Work

I have limited myself to a few of the major secondary studies for the United States and Western Europe in the post-Enlightenment period, slighting general "histories of work" when possible in favor of local studies to give the reader access to specific times and concrete historic situations. Because work is so closely interwoven in the fabric of Western social and economic history, an exhaustive list of books on how people made their living and what difference their jobs meant for their lives, would continue for thousands of titles.

Bleiber, Helmut. *Zwischen Reform und Revolution: Lage and Kämpfe der schlesischen Bauern and Landarbeiter im Vormärz, 1840–1847*. East Berlin: Akademie-Verlag, 1966.

Blumer, Herbert. "Early Industrialization and the Laboring Class." *Sociological Quarterly* 1 (1960):5–14.

Braun, Rudolf. *Industrialisierung und Volksleben: Die Veränderungen der Lebensformen in einem ländlichen Industriegebiet vor 1800 (Zürcher Oberland)*. Erlenbach-Zurich: Eugen Rentsch, 1960. A brilliant account of the arrival of cottage industry among a peasant population. For the flavor of this work see the passage translated by David Landes, ed. *The Rise of Capitalism*. New York: Macmillan, 1966, pp. 53–64.

————. *Sozialer und Kultureller Wandel in einem ländlichen Industriegebiet (Zürcher Oberland) unter Einwirkung des Maschinen- und Fabrikwesens im 19. und 20. Jahrhundert*. Erlenbach-Zurich: Eugen Rentsch, 1965.

Brown, A. F. J. *Essex at Work, 1700–1815*. Chelmsford: Essex County Council, 1969.

Bythell, Duncan. *The Handloom Weavers: A Study in the English*

*Cotton Industry during the Industrial Revolution*. New York: Cambridge University Press, 1969. Traces the economic mechanisms and political consequences of the collapse of cottage weaving.

Cole, G. D. H. *Studies in Class Structure*. London: Routledge and Kegan Paul, 1955. Important essays.

Collinet, Michel. *L'Ouvrier français: Essai sur la condition ouvrière (1900–1950)*. Paris: Editions ouvrières, 1951. Concentrates on metalworking.

Duveau, Georges. *La Vie ouvrière en France sous le Second Empire*. Paris: Gallimard, 1946. A magisterial work.

Engelsing, Rolf. "Zur politischen Bildung der deutschen Unterschichten, 1789–1863." *Historische Zeitschrift* 206 (1968):337–369. For cultural universe of servants.

Fischer, Wolfram. *Handwerksrecht und Handwerkswirtschaft um 1800: Studien zur Sozial- und Wirtschaftsverfassung vor der industriellen Revolution*. West Berlin: Duncker & Humblot, 1955.

―――. "Das deutsche Handwerk in den Frühphasen der Industrialisierung." *Zeitschrift für die Gesamte Staatswissenschaft* 120 (1964):686–712.

Garden, Maurice. *Lyon et les Lyonnais au XVIIIe siècle*. Paris: Les Belles-Lettres, 1970. Presents a careful quantitative study of the city's trades, especially of the silkweavers, highlighting social characteristics.

Giedion, Siegfried. *Mechanization Takes Command: A Contribution to Anonymous History*. New York: Oxford University Press, 1948. Eccentric but informative.

Goubert, Pierre. *Cent Mille provinciaux au XVIIe siècle: Beauvais et le Beauvaisis de 1600 à 1730*. Paris: Flammarion, 1968. An abridgement of a much larger work which was one of the first great French local studies.

Hammond, J. L. and Hammond, Barbara. *The Village Labourer*. London: Longmans, 1911.

―――. *The Town Labourer: The New Civilization, 1760–1832*. London: Longmans, 1917.

―――. *The Skilled Labourer, 1760–1832*. London: Longmans, 1919. These three volumes compose a classic series on the living conditions of English workers; all have recently reappeared in various paperback editions.

Hall, Peter G. *The Industries of London since 1861*. London: Hutchinson, 1962. Especially good on such "sweated" trades as clothing and furniture making.

Hobsbawm, E. J. *Labouring Men: Studies in the History of Labour*. New York: Basic Books, 1964. A reprinting of some of the author's fundamental essays.

Jones, Gareth Stedman. *Outcast London: A Study in the Relationship between Classes in Victorian Society*. Oxford: Clarendon Press, 1971. Centers on the casual labor market.

Kocka, Jürgen. *Unternehemsverwaltung und Angestelltenschaft am Beispiel Siemens, 1847–1914: Zum Verhältnis von Kapitalismus and Bürokratie in der deutschen Industrialisierung*. Stuttgart: Ernst Klett, 1969. A major monograph.

Krüger, Horst. *Zur Geschichte der Manufakturen und der Manufakturarbeiter in Preussen: Die mittleren Provinzen in der zweiten Hälfte des 18. Jahrhunderts*. East Berlin: Rütten & Loenig, 1958.

Kuczynski, Jürgen. *The Rise of the Working Class*. Translated by C.T.A. Ray. London: Weidenfeld and Nicolson, 1967. A short distillation of the argument running through his massive 38-volume series, "Die Geschichte der Lage der Arbeiter unter dem Kapitalismus." The author balances precariously on the line between "official" Marxism and serious historical analysis.

Landes, David. *The Unbound Prometheus: Technological Change and Industrial Development in Western Europe from 1750 to the Present*. New York: Cambridge University Press, 1969. The standard account of European industrialization; indispensable for the study of work.

Laslett, Peter. *The World We Have Lost*. 2d ed. London: Methuen, 1971. A marvelous reconstruction of the community setting of work in seventeenth-century England.

Le Roy Ladurie, Emmanuel. *Les Paysans de Languedoc*. Paris: Flammarion, 1969. Piecing together the mosaic of rural life: the condensation of a gigantic doctoral thesis.

Lewis, Brian. *Coal Mining in the Eighteenth and Nineteenth Centuries*. London: Longmans, 1971. A brief account with documents appended.

Michaud, René. *J'avais vingt ans: un jeune ouvrier au début du siècle*.

Paris: Editions syndicalistes, 1967. An unusual worker biography.

Neff, Wanda F. *Victorian Working Women: An Historical and Literary Study of Women in British Industries and Professions, 1832–1850.* London: George Allen, 1929; reprinted with a new bibliographical note. London: Frank Cass, 1966.

Musiat, Siegmund. *Zur Lebensweise des landwirtschaftlichen Gesindes in der Oberlausitz.* Bautzen: VEB Domowina, 1964. Best available work on agricultural laborers in the nineteenth century.

Pierrard, Pierre. *La Vie ouvrière à Lille sous le Second Empire.* Paris: Bloud & Gay, 1965. Massive, heavily documented.

Pollard, Sidney. *A History of Labour in Sheffield.* Liverpool: Liverpool University Press, 1959. For a sense of the differentiation among metalworking crafts.

Pinchbeck, Ivy. *Women Workers and the Industrial Revolution, 1750–1850.* London: Frank Cass, 1930. The classic study of women in the labor force.

Pope, Liston. *Millhands & Preachers: A Study of Gastonia.* New Haven, Conn.: Yale University Press, 1942. The North Carolina cotton mills in the 1920s and 1930s.

Shorter, Edward, and Tilly, Charles. *Strikes in France, 1830–1968.* New York: Cambridge University Press, 1974. How the structure of work affects the nature of militancy.

Smelser, Neil J. *Social Change in the Industrial Revolution: An Application of Theory to the British Cotton Industry.* Chicago: University of Chicago Press, 1959. Ingenious.

Smuts, Robert W. *Women and Work in America.* New York: Schocken, 1971. With a new introduction by Eli Ginzberg.

Stearns, Peter N. "Adaptation to Industrialization: German Workers as a Test Case." *Central European History* 3 (1970):303–331.

——. "Working Class Women in Britain, 1890–1914." In *Suffer and Be Still: Women in the Victorian Age,* edited by Martha Vicinus, pp. 100–120. Bloomington: Indiana University Press, 1972.

Sullerot, Evelyne. *Histoire et sociologie du travail féminin.* Paris: Gonthier, 1968. Emphasis on nineteenth and twentieth centuries.

Tardieu, Suzanne. *La Vie domestique dans le mâconnais rural préindustriel.* Paris: Institut d'ethnologie, 1964: An excellent example of an entire category of literature which brings to bear on the history of work the evidence of household artifacts.

Thernstrom, Stephan and Sennett, Richard, eds. *Nineteenth Century Cities: Essays in the New Urban History.* New Haven, Conn.: Yale University Press, 1969. Many worthwhile essays on worker life experiences, social mobility, residence, and family patterns.

Thompson, Edward P. *The Making of the English Working Class.* London: Gollancz, 1964. A powerful work on the decline of handicrafts, the rise of cottage and factory industry.

Trempé, Rolande. *Les Mineurs de Carmaux, 1848–1914.* 2 vols. Paris: Editions ouvrières, 1971. A long look through a very powerful microscope.

Vogler, Günther. *Zur Geschichte der Weber und Spinner von Nowawes, 1751–1785.* Potsdam: Bezirksheimatmuseum, 1965. The advent of cottage weaving in a village, with documents and photographs.

Walker, Mack. *German Home Towns: Community, State, and General Estate, 1648–1871.* Ithaca: Cornell University Press, 1971. Work and community in the good old days, a pioneering study.

Wiest, Ekkehard. *Die Entwicklung des Nürnberger Gewerbes zwischen 1648 und 1806.* Stuttgart: Gustav Fischer, 1968. The ins and outs of "guild" and "craft" in a quite particular time and place; thoroughly researched.

## Work in Contemporary Society

In compiling this short list I have attempted, not always successfully, to favor the "ethnology" of worker life over survey research. And I have left out almost all the literature associating industrial structure with worker organization and militancy.

Bell, Daniel. *Work and Its Discontents.* New York: League for Industrial Democracy, 1956. A provocative essay on industrial "efficiency."

Berger, Bennett M. *Working-Class Suburb: A Study of Auto Workers in Suburbia.* Berkeley and Los Angeles: University of California Press, 1960.

— Bendix, Reinhard. *Work and Authority in Industry: Ideologies of Management in the Course of Industrialization.* New York: Wiley, 1956. See on the rationalization and bureaucratization of industry.

> Blau, Peter M. and Duncan, Otis Dudley. *The American Occupational Structure.* New York: Wiley, 1967. A major empirical study linking occupation to mobility and family life.

⌐ Blauner, Robert. *Alienation and Freedom: The Factory Worker and His Industry.* Chicago: The University of Chicago Press, 1964. Survey data, thoughtfully presented on the relationship between type of work and frame of mind.

Blythe, Ronald. *Akenfield: Portrait of an English Village.* London: Allen Lane, 1969. Evokes the world of work in a small community of the twentieth century.

Braun, Rudolf. *Sozio-Kulturelle Probleme der Eingliederung italienischer Arbeitskräfte in der Schweiz.* Erlenbach-Zurich: Eugen Rentsch, 1970.

⌐ Crozier. Michel. *The Bureaucratic Phenomenon.* Translated by the author. Chicago: The University of Chicago Press, 1964. How French culture imprints the attitudes of workers in large bureaucracies.

> Dahrendorf, Ralf. *Class and Class Conflict in Industrial Society.* Stanford, Calif.: Stanford University Press, 1959. A brilliant updating of Marx.

Denis, Norman, *et al. Coal is Our Life: An Analysis of a Yorkshire Mining Community.* London: Tavistock, 1956.

Frémontier, Jacques. *La Forteresse ouvrière: Renault.* Paris: Fayard, 1971. A partisan account of work on the assembly line and its consequences for culture and organization.

Friedmann, Georges. *Industrial Society: The Emergence of the Human Problems of Automation.* Edited and with an introduction by Harold L. Sheppard. New York: Free Press, 1955. A classic text.

Gavi, Philippe. *Les Ouvriers: Du tiercé à la révolution.* Paris: Mercure de France, 1970. A journalist travels through France's industrial cities, accumulating some very sharp impressions.

Goldthorpe, John H., *et al. The Affluent Worker,* vol. I: *Industrial*

*Attitudes and Behaviour;* vol. II: *Political Attitudes and Behaviour.* New York: Cambridge University Press, 1968. Survey research on an industrial town.

Hamilton, Richard F. *Affluence and the French Worker in the Fourth Republic.* Princeton, N.J.: Princeton University Press, 1967. A secondary analysis of national survey data, finds rural roots in urban worker radicalism.

Kerr, Clark, *et al. Industrialism and Industrial Man: The Problems of Labor and Management in Economic Growth.* Cambridge, Mass.: Harvard University Press, 1960. Presents an important, but probably wrong argument about industrial change and worker militancy.

Leggett, John C. *Class, Race and Labor: Working-Class Consciousness in Detroit.* New York: Oxford University Press, 1968. A look from the left.

Lipset, Seymour Martin. "White Collar Workers and Professionals— Their Attitudes and Behavior towards Unions." In *Readings in Industrial Sociology,* edited by William A. Faunce. pp. 525–548. New York: Appleton-Century-Crofts, 1967, This volume also includes other important essays.

Lockwood, David. *The Blackcoated Worker: A Study in Class Consciousness.* London: George Allen and Unwin, 1958. Why class feeling has been slow to develop among the white-collar proletariat.

Lorimer, James and Phillips, Myfanwy. *Working People: Life in a Downtown City Neighborhood.* Toronto: James Lewis & Samuel, 1971. A collage of images of one of the few urban proletariats in North America (in Toronto) that is neither black nor in flight.

Mallet, Serge. *La Nouvelle classe ouvrière.* Paris: Seuil, 1963. The book's introduction is a major restatement of Marxist notions about the work situation and militancy.

Mills, C. Wright. *White-Collar: The American Middle Classes.* New York: Oxford University Press, 1951. A classic.

Shostak, Arthur B. *Blue-Collar Life.* New York: Random House, 1969. A first-class summary of the literature on the American working classes.

Sturmthal, Adolf, ed. *White-Collar Trade Unions: Contemporary De-*

*velopments in Industrialized Societies*. Urbana: University of Illinois Press, 1966.

Taylor, Frederick Winslow. *The Principles of Scientific Management*. 2d ed. New York: Norton, 1967. Taylor popularized efforts to rationalize shop-floor organization.

Touraine, Alain. *L'Evolution du travail ouvrier aux usines Renault*. Paris: Centre national de la recherche scientifique, 1955.

————. *La Civilisation industrielle (de 1914 à nos jours)*. Paris: Nouvelle Librairie de France, 1962; See also the other volumes in this series.

————. *Le Mouvement de mai ou le communisme utopique*. Paris: Seuil, 1968. An off-the-cuff analysis of the May 1968 general strike of French students and workers which has the brilliance of Marx's quick studies of the Paris June Days or the Commune.

————. *The Post-Industrial Society: Tomorrow's Social History: Classes, Conflicts and Culture in the Programmed Society*. Translated by Leonard F. X. Mayhew. New York: Random House, 1971. Selected essays on work, leisure, and power.

Revised January, 1970

# harper ✦ torchbooks

## American Studies: General

HENRY STEELE COMMAGER, Ed.: The Struggle for Racial Equality — TB/1300
CARL N. DEGLER: Out of Our Past: *The Forces that Shaped Modern America* — CN/2
CARL N. DEGLER, Ed.: Pivotal Interpretations of American History
Vol. I TB/1240; Vol. II TB/1241
A. S. EISENSTADT, Ed.: The Craft of American History: *Selected Essays*
Vol. I TB/1255; Vol. II TB/1256
ROBERT L. HEILBRONER: The Limits of American Capitalism — TB/1305
JOHN HIGHAM, Ed.: The Reconstruction of American History — TB/1068
ROBERT H. JACKSON: The Supreme Court in the American System of Government — TB/1106
JOHN F. KENNEDY: A Nation of Immigrants. *Illus. Revised and Enlarged. Introduction by Robert F. Kennedy* — TB/1118
RICHARD B. MORRIS: Fair Trial: *Fourteen Who Stood Accused, from Anne Hutchinson to Alger Hiss* — TB/1335
GUNNAR MYRDAL: An American Dilemma: *The Negro Problem and Modern Democracy. Introduction by the Author.*
Vol. I TB/1443; Vol. II TB/1444
GILBERT OSOFSKY, Ed.: The Burden of Race: *A Documentary History of Negro-White Relations in America* — TB/1405
ARNOLD ROSE: The Negro in America: *The Condensed Version of Gunnar Myrdal's An American Dilemma. Second Edition* TB/3048
JOHN E. SMITH: Themes in American Philosophy: *Purpose, Experience and Community* — TB/1466
WILLIAM R. TAYLOR: Cavalier and Yankee: *The Old South and American National Character* — TB/1474

## American Studies: Colonial

BERNARD BAILYN: The New England Merchants in the Seventeenth Century — TB/1149
ROBERT E. BROWN: Middle-Class Democracy and Revolution in Massachusetts, 1691–1780. *New Introduction by Author* — TB/1413
JOSEPH CHARLES: The Origins of the American Party System — TB/1049
WESLEY FRANK CRAVEN: The Colonies in Transition: 1660-1712† — TB/3084

CHARLES GIBSON: Spain in America † TB/3077
CHARLES GIBSON, Ed.: The Spanish Tradition in America + — HR/1351
LAWRENCE HENRY GIPSON: The Coming of the Revolution: 1763-1775. † *Illus.* — TB/3007
PERRY MILLER: Errand Into the Wilderness — TB/1139
PERRY MILLER & T. H. JOHNSON, Eds.: The Puritans: *A Sourcebook of Their Writings*
Vol. I TB/1093; Vol. II TB/1094
EDMUND S. MORGAN: The Puritan Family: *Religion and Domestic Relations in Seventeenth Century New England* — TB/1227
WALLACE NOTESTEIN: The English People on the Eve of Colonization: 1603-1630. † *Illus.* — TB/3006
LOUIS B. WRIGHT: The Cultural Life of the American Colonies: 1607-1763. † *Illus.* — TB/3005

## American Studies: The Revolution to 1860

JOHN R. ALDEN: The American Revolution: 1775-1783. † *Illus.* — TB/3011
RAY A. BILLINGTON: The Far Western Frontier: 1830-1860. † *Illus.* — TB/3012
GEORGE DANGERFIELD: The Awakening of American Nationalism, 1815-1828. † *Illus.* TB/3061
CLEMENT EATON: The Growth of Southern Civilization, 1790-1860. † *Illus.* — TB/3040
LOUIS FILLER: The Crusade against Slavery: 1830-1860. † *Illus.* — TB/3029
WILLIM W. FREEHLING: Prelude to Civil War: *The Nullification Controversy in South Carolina, 1816-1836* — TB/1359
THOMAS JEFFERSON: Notes on the State of Virginia. ‡ *Edited by Thomas P. Abernethy* — TB/3052
JOHN C. MILLER: The Federalist Era: 1789-1801. † *Illus.* — TB/3027
RICHARD B. MORRIS: The American Revolution Reconsidered — TB/1363
GILBERT OSOFSKY, Ed.: Puttin' On Ole Massa: *The Slave Narratives of Henry Bibb, William Wells Brown, and Solomon Northup* ‡ — TB/1432
FRANCIS S. PHILBRICK: The Rise of the West, 1754-1830. † *Illus.* — TB/3067
MARSHALL SMELSER: The Democratic Republic, 1801-1815 † — TB/1406

LOUIS B. WRIGHT: Culture on the Moving Frontier TB/1053

## American Studies: The Civil War to 1900

T. C. COCHRAN & WILLIAM MILLER: The Age of Enterprise: *A Social History of Industrial America* TB/1054
W. A. DUNNING: Reconstruction, Political and Economic: 1865-1877 TB/1073
HAROLD U. FAULKNER: Politics, Reform and Expansion: 1890-1900. † *Illus.* TB/3020
GEORGE M. FREDRICKSON: The Inner Civil War: *Northern Intellectuals and the Crisis of the Union* TB/1358
JOHN A. GARRATY: The New Commonwealth, 1877-1890 † TB/1410
HELEN HUNT JACKSON: A Century of Dishonor: *The Early Crusade for Indian Reform.* † *Edited by Andrew F. Rolle* TB/3063
WILLIAM G. MCLOUGHLIN, Ed.: The American Evangelicals, 1800-1900: An Anthology ‡ TB/1382
JAMES S. PIKE: The Prostrate State: *South Carolina under Negro Government.* ‡ *Intro. by Robert F. Durden* TB/3085
VERNON LANE WHARTON: The Negro in Mississippi, 1865-1890 TB/1178

## American Studies: The Twentieth Century

RAY STANNARD BAKER: Following the Color Line: *American Negro Citizenship in Progressive Era.* ‡ *Edited by Dewey W. Grantham, Jr. Illus.* TB/3053
RANDOLPH S. BOURNE: War and the Intellectuals: *Collected Essays, 1915-1919.* ‡ *Edited by Carl Resek* TB/3043
A. RUSSELL BUCHANAN: The United States and World War II. † *Illus.*
Vol. I TB/3044; Vol. II TB/3045
THOMAS C. COCHRAN: The American Business System: *A Historical Perspective, 1900-1955* TB/1080
FOSTER RHEA DULLES: America's Rise to World Power: 1898-1954. † *Illus.* TB/3021
HAROLD U. FAULKNER: The Decline of Laissez Faire, 1897-1917 TB/1397
JOHN D. HICKS: Republican Ascendancy: 1921-1933. † *Illus.* TB/3041
WILLIAM E. LEUCHTENBURG: Franklin D. Roosevelt and the New Deal: 1932-1940. † *Illus.* TB/3025
WILLIAM E. LEUCHTENBURG, Ed.: The New Deal: *A Documentary History* + HR/1354
ARTHUR S. LINK: Woodrow Wilson and the Progressive Era: 1910-1917. † *Illus.* TB/3023
BROADUS MITCHELL: Depression Decade: *From New Era through New Deal, 1929-1941* ∧ TB/1439
GEORGE E. MOWRY: The Era of Theodore Roosevelt and the Birth of Modern America: 1900-1912. † *Illus.* TB/3022
WILLIAM PRESTON, JR.: Aliens and Dissenters:
TWELVE SOUTHERNERS: I'll Take My Stand: *The South and the Agrarian Tradition. Intro. by Louis D. Rubin, Jr.; Biographical Essays by Virginia Rock* TB/1072

## Art, Art History, Aesthetics

ERWIN PANOFSKY: Renaissance and Renascences in Western Art. *Illus.* TB/1447
ERWIN PANOFSKY: Studies in Iconology: *Humanistic Themes in the Art of the Renaissance. 180 illus.* TB/1077
HEINRICH ZIMMER: Myths and Symbols in Indian Art and Civilization. *70 illus.* TB/2005

## Asian Studies

WOLFGANG FRANKE: China and the West: *The Cultural Encounter, 13th to 20th Centuries. Trans. by R. A. Wilson* TB/1326
L. CARRINGTON GOODRICH: A Short History of the Chinese People. *Illus.* TB/3015

## Economics & Economic History

C. E. BLACK: The Dynamics of Modernization: *A Study in Comparative History* TB/1321
GILBERT BURCK & EDITORS OF *Fortune:* The Computer Age: *And its Potential for Management* TB/1179
ROBERT L. HEILBRONER: The Future as History: *The Historic Currents of Our Time and the Direction in Which They Are Taking America* TB/1386
ROBERT L. HEILBRONER: The Great Ascent: *The Struggle for Economic Development in Our Time* TB/3030
FRANK H. KNIGHT: The Economic Organization TB/1214
DAVID S. LANDES: Bankers and Pashas: *International Finance and Economic Imperialism in Egypt. New Preface by the Author* TB/1412
ROBERT LATOUCHE: The Birth of Western Economy: *Economic Aspects of the Dark Ages* TB/1290
W. ARTHUR LEWIS: The Principles of Economic Planning. *New Introduction by the Author*° TB/1436
WILLIAM MILLER, Ed.: Men in Business: *Essays on the Historical Role of the Entrepreneur* TB/1081
HERBERT A. SIMON: The Shape of Automation: *For Men and Management* TB/1245

## Historiography and History of Ideas

J. BRONOWSKI & BRUCE MAZLISH: The Western Intellectual Tradition: *From Leonardo to Hegel* TB/3001
WILHELM DILTHEY: Pattern and Meaning in History: *Thoughts on History and Society.*° *Edited with an Intro. by H. P. Rickman* TB/1075
J. H. HEXTER: More's Utopia: *The Biography of an Idea. Epilogue by the Author* TB/1195
H. STUART HUGHES: History as Art and as Science: *Twin Vistas on the Past* TB/1207
ARTHUR O. LOVEJOY: The Great Chain of Being: *A Study of the History of an Idea* TB/1009
RICHARD H. POPKIN: The History of Scepticism from Erasmus to Descartes. *Revised Edition* TB/1391
BRUNO SNELL: The Discovery of the Mind: *The Greek Origins of European Thought* TB/1018

## History: General

HANS KOHN: The Age of Nationalism: *The First Era of Global History* TB/1380
BERNARD LEWIS: The Arabs in History TB/1029
BERNARD LEWIS: The Middle East and the West ° TB/1274

## History: Ancient

A. ANDREWS: The Greek Tyrants TB/1103
THEODOR H. GASTER: Thespis: *Ritual Myth and Drama in the Ancient Near East* TB/1281

A. H. M. JONES, Ed.: A History of Rome through the Fifth Century # *Vol. I: The Republic* HR/1364
*Vol. II The Empire:* HR/1460
SAMUEL NOAH KRAMER: Sumerian Mythology TB/1055
NAPHTALI LEWIS & MEYER REINHOLD, Eds.: Roman Civilization *Vol. I: The Republic* TB/1231
*Vol. II: The Empire* TB/1232

## History: Medieval

NORMAN COHN: The Pursuit of the Millennium: *Revolutionary Messianism in Medieval and Reformation Europe* TB/1037
F. L. GANSHOF: Feudalism TB/1058
F. L. GANSHOF: The Middle Ages: *A History of International Relations. Translated by Rémy Hall* TB/1411
HENRY CHARLES LEA: The Inquisition of the Middle Ages. || *Introduction by Walter Ullmann* TB/1456

## History: Renaissance & Reformation

JACOB BURCKHARDT: The Civilization of the Renaissance in Italy. *Introduction by Benjamin Nelson and Charles Trinkaus. Illus.* Vol. I TB/40; Vol. II TB/41
JOHN CALVIN & JACOPO SADOLETO: A Reformation Debate. *Edited by John C. Olin* TB/1239
J. H. ELLIOTT: Europe Divided, 1559-1598 α ° TB/1414
G. R. ELTON: Reformation Europe, 1517-1559 ° α TB/1270
HANS J. HILLERBRAND, Ed., The Protestant Reformation # HR/1342
JOHAN HUIZINGA: Erasmus and the Age of Reformation. *Illus.* TB/19
JOEL HURSTFIELD: The Elizabethan Nation TB/1312
JOEL HURSTFIELD, Ed.: The Reformation Crisis TB/1267
PAUL OSKAR KRISTELLER: Renaissance Thought: *The Classic, Scholastic, and Humanist Strains* TB/1048
DAVID LITTLE: Religion, Order and Law: *A Study in Pre-Revolutionary England.* § *Preface by R. Bellah* TB/1418
PAOLO ROSSI: Philosophy, Technology, and the Arts, in the Early Modern Era 1400-1700. || *Edited by Benjamin Nelson. Translated by Salvator Attanasio* TB/1458
H. R. TREVOR-ROPER: The European Witch-craze of the Sixteenth and Seventeenth Centuries and Other Essays ° TB/1416

## History: Modern European

ALAN BULLOCK: Hitler, A Study in Tyranny. ° *Revised Edition. Illus.* TB/1123
JOHANN GOTTLIEB FICHTE: Addresses to the German Nation. *Ed. with Intro. by George A. Kelly* ¶ TB/1366
ALBERT GOODWIN: The French Revolution TB/1064
STANLEY HOFFMANN et al.: In Search of France. *The Economy, Society and Political System In the Twentieth Century* TB/1219
H. STUART HUGHES: The Obstructed Path: *French Social Thought in the Years of Desperation* TB/1451
JOHAN HUIZINGA: Dutch Civilisation in the 17th Century and Other Essays TB/1453

JOHN MCMANNERS: European History, 1789-1914: *Men, Machines and Freedom* TB/1419
HUGH SETON-WATSON: Eastern Europe Between the Wars, 1918-1941 TB/1330
ALBERT SOREL: Europe Under the Old Regime. *Translated by Francis H. Herrick* TB/1121
A. J. P. TAYLOR: From Napoleon to Lenin: *Historical Essays "* TB/1268
A. J. P. TAYLOR: The Habsburg Monarchy, 1809-1918: *A History of the Austrian Empire and Austria-Hungary* ° TB/1187
J. M. THOMPSON: European History, 1494-1789 TB/1431
H. R. TREVOR-ROPER: Historical Essays TB/1269

## Literature & Literary Criticism

W. J. BATE: From Classic to Romantic: *Premises of Taste in Eighteenth Century England* TB/1036
VAN WYCK BROOKS: Van Wyck Brooks: The Early Years: *A Selection from his Works, 1908-1921 Ed. with Intro. by Claire Sprague* TB/3082
RICHMOND LATTIMORE, Translator: The Odyssey of Homer TB/1389
ROBERT PREYER, Ed.: Victorian Literature ** TB/1302

## Philosophy

HENRI BERGSON: Time and Free Will: *An Essay on the Immediate Data of Consciousness* ° TB/1021
H. J. BLACKHAM: Six Existentialist Thinkers: *Kierkegaard, Nietzsche, Jaspers, Marcel, Heidegger, Sartre* ° TB/1002
J. M. BOCHENSKI: The Methods of Contemporary Thought. *Trans. by Peter Caws* TB/1377
ERNST CASSIRER: Rousseau, Kant and Goethe. *Intro. by Peter Gay* TB/1092
MICHAEL GELVEN: A Commentary on Heidegger's "Being and Time" TB/1464
J. GLENN GRAY: Hegel and Greek Thought TB/1409
W. K. C. GUTHRIE: The Greek Philosophers: *From Thales to Aristotle* ° TB/1008
G. W. F. HEGEL: Phenomenology of Mind. ° || *Introduction by George Lichtheim* TB/1303
MARTIN HEIDEGGER: Discourse on Thinking. *Translated with a Preface by John M. Anderson and E. Hans Freund. Introduction by John M. Anderson* TB/1459
F. H. HEINEMANN: Existentialism and the Modern Predicament TB/28
WERER HEISENBERG: Physics and Philosophy: *The Revolution in Modern Science. Intro. by F. S. C. Northrop* TB/549
EDMUND HUSSERL: Phenomenology and the Crisis of Philosophy. § *Translated with an Introduction by Quentin Lauer* TB/1170
IMMANUEL KANT: Groundwork of the Metaphysic of Morals. *Translated and Analyzed by H. J. Paton* TB/1159
WALTER KAUFMANN, Ed.: Religion From Tolstoy to Camus: *Basic Writings on Religious Truth and Morals* TB/123
QUENTIN LAUER: Phenomenology: *Its Genesis and Prospect. Preface by Aron Gurwitsch* TB/1169
MICHAEL POLANYI: Personal Knowledge: *Towards a Post-Critical Philosophy* TB/1158
WILLARD VAN ORMAN QUINE: Elementary Logic *Revised Edition* TB/577
WILHELM WINDELBAND: A History of Philosophy *Vol. I: Greek, Roman, Medieval* TB/38

Vol. II: Renaissance, Enlightenment, Modern TB/39
LUDWIG WITTGENSTEIN: The Blue and Brown Books ° TB/1211
LUDWIG WITTGENSTEIN: Notebooks, 1914-1916 TB/1441

## Political Science & Government

C. E. BLACK: The Dynamics of Modernization: A Study in Comparative History TB/1321
DENIS W. BROGAN: Politics in America. New Introduction by the Author TB/1469
ROBERT CONQUEST: Power and Policy in the USSR: The Study of Soviet Dynastics ° TB/1307
JOHN B. MORRALL: Political Thought in Medieval Times TB/1076
KARL R. POPPER: The Open Society and Its Enemies Vol. I: The Spell of Plato TB/1101
Vol. II: The High Tide of Prophecy: Hegel, Marx, and the Aftermath TB/1102
HENRI DE SAINT-SIMON: Social Organization, The Science of Man, and Other Writings. || Edited and Translated with an Introduction by Felix Markham TB/1152
CHARLES SCHOTTLAND, Ed.: The Welfare State ** TB/1323
JOSEPH A. SCHUMPETER: Capitalism, Socialism and Democracy TB/3008

## Psychology

LUDWIG BINSWANGER: Being-in-the-World: Selected Papers. || Trans. with Intro. by Jacob Needleman TB/1365
MIRCEA ELIADE: Cosmos and History: The Myth of the Eternal Return § TB/2050
MIRCEA ELIADE: Myth and Reality TB/1369
SIGMUND FREUD: On Creativity and the Unconscious: Papers on the Psychology of Art, Literature, Love, Religion. § Intro. by Benjamin Nelson TB/45
J. GLENN GRAY: The Warriors: Reflections on Men in Battle. Introduction by Hannah Arendt TB/1294
WILLIAM JAMES: Psychology: The Briefer Course. Edited with an Intro. by Gordon Allport TB/1034

## Religion: Ancient and Classical, Biblical and Judaic Traditions

MARTIN BUBER: Eclipse of God: Studies in the Relation Between Religion and Philosophy TB/12
MARTIN BUBER: Hasidism and Modern Man. Edited and Translated by Maurice Friedman TB/839
MARTIN BUBER: The Knowledge of Man. Edited with an Introduction by Maurice Friedman. Translated by Maurice Friedman and Ronald Gregor Smith TB/135
MARTIN BUBER: Moses. The Revelation and the Covenant TB/837
MARTIN BUBER: The Origin and Meaning of Hasidism. Edited and Translated by Maurice Friedman TB/835
MARTIN BUBER: The Prophetic Faith TB/73
MARTIN BUBER: Two Types of Faith: Interpenetration of Judaism and Christianity ° TB/75
M. S. ENSLIN: Christian Beginnings TB/5
M. S. ENSLIN: The Literature of the Christian Movement TB/6
HENRI FRANKFORT: Ancient Egyptian Religion: An Interpretation TB/77

## Religion: Early Christianity Through Reformation

ANSELM OF CANTERBURY: Truth, Freedom, and Evil: Three Philosophical Dialogues. Edited and Translated by Jasper Hopkins and Herbert Richardson TB/317
EDGAR J. GOODSPEED: A Life of Jesus TB/1
ROBERT M. GRANT: Gnosticism and Early Christianity TB/136

## Religion: Oriental Religions

TOR ANDRAE: Mohammed: The Man and His Faith § TB/62
EDWARD CONZE: Buddhism: Its Essence and Development. ° Foreword by Arthur Waley TB/58
H. G. CREEL: Confucius and the Chinese Way TB/63
FRANKLIN EDGERTON, Trans. & Ed.: The Bhagavad Gita TB/115
SWAMI NIKHILANANDA, Trans. & Ed.: The Upanishads TB/114
D. T. SUZUKI: On Indian Mahayana Buddhism. ° Ed. with Intro. by Edward Conze. TB/1403

## Science and Mathematics

W. E. LE GROS CLARK: The Antecedents of Man: An Introduction to the Evolution of the Primates. ° Illus. TB/559
ROBERT E. COKER: Streams, Lakes, Ponds. Illus. TB/586
ROBERT E. COKER: This Great and Wide Sea: An Introduction to Oceanography and Marine Biology. Illus. TB/551
WILLARD VAN ORMAN QUINE: Mathematical Logic TB/558

## Sociology and Anthropology

REINHARD BENDIX: Work and Authority in Industry: Ideologies of Management in the Course of Industrialization TB/3035
KENNETH B. CLARK: Dark Ghetto: Dilemmas of Social Power. Foreword by Gunnar Myrdal TB/1317
KENNETH CLARK & JEANNETTE HOPKINS: A Relevant War Against Poverty: A Study of Community Action Programs and Observable Social Change TB/1480
LEWIS COSER, Ed.: Political Sociology TB/1293
GARY T. MARX: Protest and Prejudice: A Study of Belief in the Black Community TB/1435
ROBERT K. MERTON, LEONARD BROOM, LEONARD S. COTTRELL, JR., Editors: Sociology Today: Problems and Prospects ||
Vol. I TB/1173; Vol. II TB/1174
GILBERT OSOFSKY, Ed.: The Burden of Race: A Documentary History of Negro-White Relations in America TB/1405
GILBERT OSOFSKY: Harlem: The Making of a Ghetto: Negro New York 1890-1930 TB/1381
PHILIP RIEFF: The Triumph of the Therapeutic: Uses of Faith After Freud TB/1360
ARNOLD ROSE: The Negro in America: The Condensed Version of Gunnar Myrdal's An American Dilemma. Second Edition TB/3048
GEORGE ROSEN: Madness in Society: Chapters in the Historical Sociology of Mental Illness. || Preface by Benjamin Nelson TB/1337
PITIRIM A. SOROKIN: Contemporary Sociological Theories: Through the First Quarter of the Twentieth Century TB/3046
FLORIAN ZNANIECKI: The Social Role of the Man of Knowledge. Introduction by Lewis A. Coser TB/1372